Number's Up

Number's Up

A Barrow Bay Mystery — Book 1

Annabelle Hunter

Number's Up

Barrow Bay Mysteries Book 1

Copyright 2019 by Annabelle Hunter

https://annabellehunter.com/

This is a work of fiction. Any resemblance to real or actual persons, places or events is completely coincidental.

Cover Design by Melody Simmons

Editing by Casey Harris-Parks of Heart Full of Ink

Proof Editing by Josh Stabile

ISBN: 978-1-7330325-4-4 (Book)

ISBN: 978-1-7330325-3-7 (ebook)

Version: 7.31.19

CHECK OUT THESE OTHER WORKS BY ANNABELLE HUNTER

Lark Davis Mystery

Leg Up

Stir Up

Load Up - To be released in September 2019

Barrow Bay Mysteries

Number's Up

DEDICATION

This book is dedicated to my husband, who keeps letting me do this, even though he sighs when he sees the bills. I love you, sweetie.

ACKNOWLEDGMENTS

Thank you to all the people who have encouraged me and helped me along this journey:

First to my friends, who supported me with love, support, and a willingness to read. I would be nowhere without them. Especially my newest friends, the fabulous authors and writers that have helped me find the right word or right path. Calmed me down when I freaked out. Nikol and Andra, you two have been amazing, and I couldn't have done this without you. Thank you, thank you, thank you.

Then to all the people that were willing to read and give me their feedback. I have found great friends, writers, and authors through this experience, and I thank you all for every time you were honest with me, even when it meant that you might hurt my feelings. And every compliment. I like those, too.

I'd also like to thank my editor, Casey Harris-Parks, for all her patience, time, and humor. Thank you for making me better, for always pushing for just a little bit more, and for truly being there when I needed someone to lean on.

And as always, I would like to thank my family for helping and encouraging me and being so excited that I was taking this step.

CHAPTER 1

I had ruined my life.

Which was a problem, because I, Jennifer Ward, MBA, CPA, and business consultant, liked my life.

The minute I opened my door to a giant in an FBI coat holding up a piece of paper, along with a black, square-shaped object that he flipped open and then closed again, I knew it. I blinked and both were gone, but I assumed from the paper I couldn't rip my eyes away from, it was a badge.

An FBI agent plus a warrant? Yep. I had ruined my life. Stupid morals. Why had I reported them? Was it really the right thing? Yes. Insider trading was a big deal. And illegal. And that mattered to me, no matter how much it destroyed everything I had built.

"Jennifer Ward?" He waited for my nod before continuing, "My name is Special Agent Nicholas Kelly. I'm with the FBI. We have a warrant to search your house and office." He scanned me before one eyebrow lifted. Just like Spock from *Star Trek*. Well, if Spock had been a six-foot-six brunet with hazel eyes and powerful shoulders that looked like he would fit in on the field of some sport. Damn. I was not going to admit how sexy

1

that was. "Also, as much as I appreciate the view, it might help if you put on more clothing."

This was a learning experience. Leggings and a camisole without a bra didn't cut it for the FBI investigative team. Any other time, I would have appreciated him letting me change. Today? Today, I was too mortified to think rationally, which was my excuse for snapping back.

"I'm sorry I didn't dress to impress. What's the normal dress code for letting the FBI search my house and home office? An orange jumpsuit and a straitjacket?" *Oh, please don't let my lawyer hear that I said that. He might fire me as a client right then and there.*

He took another long look, running his eyes up and down me as he thought, his lips twitching slightly upwards. I had amused him.

I ignored the tingles his gaze caused, focusing on my disapproving frown instead. I was not going to find someone like him attractive. Nope. With a ready smirk, relaxed stance, and confidence seeping out of every pore, here stood a charmer, a lady's man, a rake. I had gone out with bad boys before and this man was their king. He probably had plenty of girls at every stop. Ones he never thought of after he was gone. I didn't need another playboy. They were never as much fun as I always hoped. This giant version was not going to make me crack. I wanted a nice man. Responsible. Faithful. That was what I was looking for. Someone loyal and boring.

"Well, I don't think orange would be your color, but it's your choice." Then he stopped, his eyes stuck south of my face, a slight ring of red coming to his cheeks. "Yeah, I would definitely recommend changing."

I looked down and ran away. Tingles and no bra were a bad combo. Abandoning the door since I couldn't stop him and any other agent with him anyway, I made a beeline to my bedroom, because a bra was needed, and it was needed now. I made sure the door was closed before I took off my camisole, grabbing underwear and a more conservative blouse from my closet.

Why was everything I owned fashionable and form-fitting? I didn't want to be cute right now. I wanted to be... was there a word for unattractive without actually being unattractive? If not, there should be. Unisex? No, that wasn't right.

"I can't actually have you in the house without supervision. You might be destroying evidence in there," came the deep voice through the door.

"You open that door and I may have to kill you."

He wouldn't open that door. Would he? I froze, staring at the knob, praying that it didn't open before I got my shirt on.

Shit. If I had limited time to get dressed, freezing was the wrong call. I pulled the professional button-up blue shirt over my head, sweeping my hair into a messy bun instead of brushing it into a neat ponytail and jumped to the door, swinging it open before he could.

He was on the other side grinning at me. "You know, threatening a federal agent is against the law."

"I'll take my chances," I muttered back. "What do you want?" *Stupid question.* I stood behind it anyways.

"We have a warrant to search your home and office for evidence of insider trading from one of your clients."

Today's federal agents were a gift from Tony Harris himself. I would have to thank Tony with a basket of snakes the next time I saw him. Non-poisonous ones, of course. I wasn't stupid enough to kill him. Just maim him a little. Tony Harris was a horrible man that my firm had been representing for years, up until a few months ago, when we dropped him due to conflicts with his business account.

Those conflicts really had been me, not that I told my business partner, Henry, that. Finding out that Tony had been doing insider trading and that my partner had been covering it up had really broken my trust. As far as I knew, no one had found out who'd reported it in the first place.

No one knew I had betrayed them.

No. I *reported* them. It wasn't betrayal. It was morally right. It just felt like betrayal.

I needed to clean something. Anything. There had to be something to clean. There wasn't, not that the agents would let me, anyway.

"Fine." My lawyer had been very clear on this point. *Don't bother the federal agents. Let them look at anything they wanted to.* But that didn't mean I couldn't try to maintain some control. Maybe I could try to protect my other customers a little bit. "Tell me what files you want—"

"Not how this works, sweetheart. You sit over in the living room and I will be over to interview you."

Sweetheart? Oh, no. Uh-uh, nay, nope, negative, vetoed.

I could feel my face turn hot, but I pressed my lips together to keep anything stupid from coming out of my mouth. I was a professional. I could stay calm and respectful.

I would just let him know that I would not be condescended to like that. Not in my home. I didn't care if he was a six-foot-six giant of a man with the most beautiful hazel eyes that I had ever seen. They started out blue on the outside, before a starburst of brown exploded in the center, spreading out like someone had spilled golden paint—

No. He was condescending. A bad boy. And he thought that I might be a criminal. He was not a dating prospect.

Also, I would not be relegated to the couch as his team of… of… *people* came in and… did their job. That rant went downhill quickly. It didn't matter. I was still angry. I wasn't going to let logic stop me. My life was going down in self-created flames. And I needed someone to blame for it.

"I will not be told to sit down like I'm a criminal." Again, maybe that wasn't the best argument. Since my business partner might have been a criminal, and all. "Fine. I will wait in the living room." No, that was too easy for him. I couldn't let it go like that. "After I make some tea."

"Some tea?" he asked, his head tilted to the side slightly. "What kind of tea?"

"Like you care." I stomped away, trying not to notice that he was following instead of meeting with the other FBI agents mingling around my house. No, refusing to notice was passive, and I was not passive. I was just going to ignore him following me. Actively.

I was attempting not to obsess over the fact that I didn't let them in. I had lost control of our business and now my own house. I clenched my hands to stop myself from kicking them out. Restoring order. No, right now the only control I had was over myself, and I was going to be fabulous at that. I was going to stay in control. No matter what.

I was not going to worry that they were moving my stuff. Although, now that I noticed, I had to admit they were moving it very carefully, searching through items before putting them back in place where they found them.

Which was weird, right? I mean, on TV shows, the police and federal agents would tear everything apart trying to find the missing information. The people in my house were polite. Yes, they were going through my stuff, but slowly. Methodically. Then returning it to nearly the same condition.

It was weird. Appreciated, but weird.

But still, I hadn't let them in. They just came in.

Court-approved entry. They were in charge. I was in hell.

Making it to the kitchen, I pulled out my loose leaf tea pot brewer, the one that had the tea in the center and heated the water to the perfect temperature based on the type, and started putting together a cup of my vanilla

Ceylon tea. Hmm, I hadn't worked out today. Maybe I should go light on the sugar? I loved my curves, but currently I was a little too curvy, right around my waist.

"What kind of tea is that?" he asked, staring at the brewer with his nostrils flaring as he inhaled the scent from where he stood.

He was going to make fun of my tea, I just knew it. He was probably a coffee drinker. I looked him up and down. Black. I was willing to bet he drank coffee black; sugar and crème being too wussy for an agent like him.

"Does it matter?" Scratch the diet. I could already tell that this was not a diet day. Extra sugar. Maybe it would improve my mood. Sugar makes me happy and happy people don't kill FBI agents. Yep, I was sacrificing my diet so I wouldn't go to jail.

"I guess it doesn't. I was just curious." He meandered through my kitchen, picking up things and then putting them down. Because that wasn't obnoxious to someone who liked control as much as I did.

"I don't have any evidence in here," I snapped. I needed to calm down. Calm and professional. It was expected that they would look around my house. This was their job. This wasn't their fault; it was Henry's for helping to commit a crime.

And maybe a little of mine for betraying and turning in my mentor and business partner for that crime.

I turned to face the counter as my heart constricted in my chest. No, I had done the right thing. It wasn't my fault. Mostly.

"Probably not. I was just getting to know you a little more."

"And what have you figured out?"

"Workaholic, but I knew that from your work hours. Neat freak." He nodded around the room, pointing out that everything was in its place, every dish cleaned. "Single, and from the look of the book collection, chronically so."

I felt my face flush at his last statement. Yes, I was chronically single. My last boyfriend was a huge, cheating, man-whore mistake that I tried not to think about, and Barrow Bay wasn't the best place to try to attract a man. I looked at the self-help dating books he referenced. I knew how many there were. Six. Six times that I had decided to take my own happiness by the horns and find the love I wanted. I had failed. No, it was worse— I'd barely tried.

The real problem was that I worked too much. It was hard to compete with girls that actually remembered their accounts and responded back when it came to online dating. I would get lost in work and forget to respond. A lot. It was almost as bad as how often I forgot to buy groceries. I looked around. Which I hadn't done this week, either.

"Hmm, no protest?" He watched me closely, waiting for an outburst.

I wasn't going to give him the satisfaction. I bit my lips closed and held myself still, not giving an inch.

"Contained." He took a step towards me, meeting my eyes with a slight smile. "Meticulous." Another step. "Detailed." Another. "Passionate." His voice trailed off as his last step took him next to me, his body inches away from mine. I lifted my chin so I could keep his gaze. "About your job. The perfect accountant." His voice had lowered to a whisper. I was slightly dazed by his proximity.

Why was he so close?

He leaned closer to speak into my ear, his breath sending shivers down my spine. "I don't trust perfection. It's always hiding something. What are you hiding? Are you as morally bankrupt as your partner? Does your pretty face hide a black heart?"

I was so focused on his body and his breath that it took me a moment to understand what he said. He stayed next to me after he asked his question, holding me in his spell for a second longer than I should have allowed. He smelled so good. Spices and musk. I couldn't stop myself from taking a deep breath before the moment broke.

"What?" Did he say I had a black heart?

Was he… did he just try to seduce me in my own kitchen? While his team looked through my house? For a confession? How. *Dare*. He.

I opened my mouth to lay into him.

Ding.

He lifted a finger to tell me to wait while he answered his phone.

Did he just…? And I actually stopped…? No.

"Nic," he grunted into the phone.

I watched as he nodded a few times, listening to the person on the other side of the phone.

"Right. I'll be there in a few." He hung up and turned to me. "I have to go, sweetheart, but I'll be back."

"Don't call me 'sweetheart,'" I ground out between my teeth as he began walking away.

"Why? Are you not sweet?" He sent me a smirk over his shoulder.

"Because you will never find out." My teeth were clenched so tightly that my jaw hurt, but I hadn't cracked completely. "Those of us with hidden *black hearts* are picky about who we let taste us."

Oh my god. That sounded better and way less dirty in my head. *Way* less dirty. Like, epically less dirty. Shit.

His smirk spread over his face. He turned and walked back to me, crowding me once again to see if I would take a step back.

I didn't.

I should have, but I didn't.

"You, *sweetheart*, might be worth the taste. Also, you might want to clear out while we search. It's going to be a while. We can do the interview later." Then he spun around and left.

He was everything I was taught Satan would be. Temptation wrapped in a package that would destroy me if I took the bait. So I wouldn't.

I hadn't backed down. But I didn't think I'd won that battle.

Chapter 2

Three weeks later

Seven weeks ago, I turned in a confidential tip to the authorities alerting them to possible insider trading.

Three weeks ago, the FBI tore my business apart looking for evidence of insider trading. Evidence they found. Evidence I knew they would find. Because I was a great CPA. When I made an accusation, I knew it would stick. No matter how much I might've wished I was wrong.

Two weeks ago, the scandal broke, and we started to lose customers.

I stared at the spreadsheet in front of me, rubbing my temple with my left hand.

Numbers. Seven, three, two. They were all numbers. Innocent, ambivalent numbers.

Usually, I liked numbers. Numbers were unchanging and consistent. They couldn't disappoint you because they just were. But mine were not good. Seventy percent of our business had left. Almost all of Henry's clients, which was good since he had taken a voluntary sabbatical after the FBI raid on his offices.

His raid went worse than mine, and mine included a dead horse and being kidnapped, so that was saying something. Either way, the business was failing.

I was failing.

It turned out I had been wrong all these years. Numbers could disappoint. Or maybe I was just disappointed in myself.

Nah, I was going to blame the numbers for a little while longer. Then I'd own up to the obvious.

My business was failing and I had been the instrument in my own downfall. I snorted. How biblical. I should get the pastor to do a sermon about that on Sunday. He was usually good for a few inspirational quotes and I could use all the inspiration he was willing to deal out this week.

I stared at the numbers again. Maybe I had made the wrong decision trying to keep the business open after the scandal broke. As far as I knew, no one had been arrested yet, but freezing Tony Harris's accounts had been a red flag to the bulls of the business community. Harris Industries had been the first company to pull their business, although Tiffany, Tony's sister and the head of Harris Industries, had been apologetic. She even offered me a job if I wanted to close down this business and move to the city. I hadn't been that desperate at the time.

I was getting there.

Since the numbers weren't changing, no matter how much I tried to wish them into the black, I instead thought about opening up my wine early. Maybe my beer-goggles, or in this case, wine-goggles, would make the numbers look better than they were.

The knock on my door brought me out of my calculation of how many new customers I would have to bring in. I didn't normally bring in new customers, that had been Henry's job. My job was to make sure that they stayed. Bringing in new customers meant travel and meeting new people. I didn't like meeting new people. Heck, outside of this town, I didn't like meeting people period. But I disliked not having a job more, so I was going to have to figure it out.

Or close the company down.

No. I wasn't ready to do that. I looked down at the papers in my hand one last time and decided everything could wait for tomorrow. The knock meant it was time to drink.

Here's to ignoring my issues and drowning my spreadsheets.

"Hold on, Lark. Give me a second to put this away and I'll be right out," I called out, carefully placing the papers back in their folders and shutting down my computer.

Knock. Knock.

That was weird. Lark, my best friend, never knocked twice. To that point, Lark only knocked when she was too excited to ring the doorbell.

"Coming," I yelled a little louder. Maybe it was one of my neighbors. Like most of Barrow Bay, my neighbors had an average age of sixty, most having hearing issues of some type, and an intense hatred of hearing aids. I hoped their inability to hear would be in my favor one day. *If I ever dated again, that is.*

Walking out of the office, I made sure that everything was put away neatly in its assigned place. Control. Organization. They were the keys to getting me through the day. My best friend from college had been the opposite. Her side of the room had always been a mess of items stacked too high and clothing piles. But she somehow knew where everything was. After one semester, we agreed to never live together again. We still stayed best friends, until I moved here and got too busy to reach out more than a few times a year.

Finally reaching the door, I opened it.

"Lark? What's up with all the… Satan."

"Hello, Jen. Can I come in and talk to you?" Like last time, he flashed his badge. Since I wasn't focused on a warrant this time, I did manage to see a photo, but not much more. It couldn't be that I was too focused on his picture to read it. Nope. Couldn't be that at all.

"But it's been three weeks." This couldn't be happening. Had they found something else? We couldn't have had another dirty client. No.

"Counting down the days since you last saw me, were you?" He raised one brow.

There he went again with the eyebrow thing. *No.* I couldn't find that sexy. Even after everything that had happened, I couldn't deny that Special Agent Nicholas Kelly was hot. Cliché-of-steaming-playboy hot.

"It's been weeks. It's over. Done with. Nothing more here. You caught your guy. I have nothing else for you to invade." I blinked at him, trying to process what his presence could mean. And, more to the point, what I had just said. Invade? My mouth, however, didn't process. It just kept going, letting all my thoughts out for the agent to hear. "Wait. Maybe you need to talk to me to close out the case? Perfect. Case closed. Thanks for coming, bye." I tried to close the door, but Special Agent Satan stopped me.

"One, it's only been three weeks, not a month. And no, that's not why I'm here." His hand rested on the frame, stopping me from being able to close the door all the way without smashing his hand. Not good. I was pretty sure that smooshing a federal agent's hand might count as felony assault. On the other hand, felony assault couldn't have too much jail time associated with it. Right?

"Okay. Then what brings a—" I trailed off. Insult. Insult. I needed an insult, ASAP. I already used Satan. And Special Agent Ass Hat was so last visit.

"FBI agent," he supplied.

Damn. If I had anything better, I would go with it, but I didn't.

"—*Satan* to my doorstep?" When not creative, go with a classic.

"You reported Tony Harris, didn't you?" That sounded almost accusatory.

Was he mad that the tip came from me?

Also, I didn't know if I wanted to admit that. I paused, struggling to remember what my lawyer had said to do if they showed up again. I could remember throwing away the note with his instructions three days ago, but that wasn't helpful. Why hadn't I reread it before throwing it away? Pains of being a neat freak.

To make matters worse, I couldn't remember what I had admitted to the last time they were here. I was pretty angry and a little panicked at the time. It didn't matter that I had known they might come. Having the FBI here, in my house, was nerve-racking. It was like I was constantly on guard, waiting for them to find something that I knew they weren't going to find. Like when a police officer drove behind me. It didn't matter that I was going the speed limit, and following all of the laws. I stressed. And this man in front of me had not helped. In fact, he had kept me in a constant state of defensive anger.

The only thing that had been worse than his behavior was my own anxiety going crazy every time he left me alone. It had been a sucky few days. But that was in the past. I needed to focus on the here and now.

"I don't know what you're talking about," I responded quickly, crossing my arms over my chest. "You already have everything. Got the warrant and searched the whole house. Even my kitchen." I glared extra hard on that one. I hadn't forgotten his comment when we met the first time. I had never been accused of having a black heart before. Or been told I was pretty in quite such an annoying way. "Why are you here now?"

"You never asked why we came last time." He leaned against the doorway, studying me. "You just opened your doors and let us in. Also, you hired a lawyer a week before the tip." He smiled at me, smugly.

I sighed. I knew that was going to come back to bite me. I had hired a lawyer before I even submitted the tip, even though I knew it would look bad, but I wanted to make sure I was protected. As my business partner was probably in on the whole thing, the lawyer and I hadn't known if he could do much more than save my license, but he was willing to try. The good news was that he was now sure I would still have my license. Silver linings and all that.

I needed to come up with a distraction because I didn't know where this was going, which worried me. And, frankly, I was having enough nightmares over my business issues. I didn't need this on top of it.

"What do you want? I don't have any of Harris's records in my home office. I turned over everything when I dropped him as a client. Not to mention, your group already looked. Plus, isn't he in jail?" Because that would be nice. I could use an end to this whole thing.

He recoiled slightly at my hostile tone. I hadn't realized he knew how to back down from a challenge. It made me feel slightly victorious.

"We wanted to look around again anyway." He pulled up to his full height to intimidate me, but I was too distracted to care.

Wow. Evidently, I looked like I was born yesterday. "Do you have another warrant?"

"We were hoping that you would cooperate without dragging your name into the court system—" He smirked. "—again."

Damn. He had a point. I *didn't* want my name in the court system again. The first time with the first warrant was enough.

"Still no. I have a responsibility to my clients." What few I had left. "Please return with a warrant."

I hated being responsible. Some days it was all downside and very little up.

"You know, not many girls turn me down." He leaned more against the doorframe, but still didn't move the hand preventing me from closing the door. I checked.

"That's because you have been talking to girls. You might try women and let me know how many 'no's you get then." I bared my teeth in what I hoped might be mistaken as a smile.

His grin faltered, but he continued on. "Are you sure I can't come in and ask you some questions?" He moved closer to me, pressing into my personal space. "Maybe get to know you a little better? We got off to a bad start last time."

I expected better. That was proof he had been flying by his good looks too long.

"No."

"No?" he repeated, his eyebrows raising slightly in surprise.

How did people treat these men outside of Barrow Bay? Did women just let attractive men walk all over them? Because Lark's boyfriend Brecken had this issue, too. It was like they couldn't conceive that we might not be willing to lay down and let them walk all over us.

"Nope. Because once you're in here, you're going to make small talk before you need to 'go to the bathroom.' Then you'll help yourself to a little look around my house. So, no."

"I'm a federal agent." He did look mildly offended. Or he was acting.

I couldn't tell.

"I know. You've flashed me something that could have been a badge." I waved at him, indicating how fast it had gone by.

"*Could* have been?"

"It went by pretty fast. It really could have been anything." I shrugged. "I don't actually remember seeing it last time either."

"Do you want me to flash you again?"

Yes, but maybe not the badge. My eyes dropped down before I could stop them, and he smiled even wider.

Yep. He saw that. Damn.

"No."

Nic's -- I mean Nicholas's -- smirk covered his whole face. "That look said—"

"Jen?" Lark's voice cut through whatever Nic was about to say. "Is something wrong?" She walked up the path, carrying a bag from the local grocery. Hopefully it was more wine. I didn't think the one bottle in the fridge would be enough anymore.

"No. Everything's *fine*. Nicholas was just *leaving*." I glared at him, trying to force him away with my ire. He held for a second before pulling his hand back, giving me a slight frown. One echoed by Lark, who was not happy that Nic had shown up again after the last visit. They hadn't exactly gotten along. Or maybe I hadn't gotten along and she just backed me up.

No, she named him Mr. Unimportant before she knew I knew him. I was going to vote she wasn't a fan.

"Have it your way. I'll see you again soon." Nic turned, but still hesitated, like he wanted to say something else.

Great. I was definitely going to have nightmares tonight. Starring a sexy, brown-haired Spock. Who didn't actually look anything like Spock. I didn't know why that kept coming to my mind. Whatever the reason, it stopped now.

"Well, then. Have a great night." I slammed the door in his face.

That was stupid. Lark was still out there. I had to open the door again. This was so embarrassing.

Then again, I had always wanted to slam a door in someone's face. I couldn't lie. It had felt good.

Sighing, I opened the door again to find Lark staring down an amused Nicholas.

"Did you stand her up? Because we don't like men who make promises and then don't follow through around here." Lark moved into his space, hitting him with her best glare and wagging her finger. Just like her grandmother. Oh my gosh. She was going to die when I told her.

"No. No, I didn't stand her up."

"Jen likes everyone but you. Somehow, she's always angry at you. What did you do?"

I did *not* like everyone. And she knew it. But I had to admit, the point was better when she said it like that.

"I assure you Jen likes me fine."

No, I didn't. I might be slightly attracted, but I did not like him.

"You shouldn't make conclusions you can't support." I told him before turning to Lark. "Ignore him. He's just here for business."

Larks eyebrows met her hairline as she stared at me. "Did they find something new?"

Satan groaned. "No one's talking about an ongoing case to an unrelated civilian," he told both of us, sending me a warning glance. "Lark. A pain, as always," he joked as he turned to leave.

I was not sure what he thought I knew that Lark didn't, but whatever.

"How do you stand this guy? Is it because he's hot? Because that isn't a good reason to let someone into your house."

"Oh my god, Lark. You can't say things like that in front of people." And I didn't stand him. I just found him irrationally sexy. And one-upping him was kind of fun. Plus, he had been leaving until she said that. Now, he had stopped and turned back.

"Please. Look at his cocky smile. That man knows he's attractive and uses it."

"He's no Captain America," I agreed. Lark had started talking with her self-proclaimed, not-boyfriend, Brecken (aka Captain America), seven weeks ago when he helped solve a murder she was involved in. He was a detective down in San Francisco, which was about an hour-and-a-half drive away from here. As she had just gotten out of a bad divorce two years prior and he was a workaholic, they were taking it slow. Really slow. I didn't know how she did it. The man looked like he walked off the set of the Marvel movies. Her own real-life Captain America. Mouth-wateringly gorgeous. I would've jumped him by now if I had been her. "And notice that he isn't in my house, in fact he's just *leaving*."

"I always liked Wolverine more," Nicholas mused, ignoring my comment completely.

Lark turned to study him.

"Yeah, you do have the whole Wolverine thing going. Broody and relentless. But Jen needs a real hero, not an anti-hero working on the side of good. So, you can go." She turned and dismissed him as he stared, his chin hanging low. He was obviously not used to people getting the better of him. That was probably why Lark irked him.

"I love you," I told her as she came through the door. I closed it before he could recover.

"Because I'm awkward and say everything that comes to mind?"

"Pretty much."

"So, are you going to tell me what that was about?"

"I don't know. He didn't tell me why the case brought him back. He just asked to take another look around." I sighed. "I need to call my lawyer. Again." And be charged for his advice.

Lawyer was the right word to use because after that Lark found a new topic.

"I got three more bottles of wine."

"Three?" That wasn't a good sign.

On the other hand, that meant two bottles for her and two for me. So much better than the one bottle for both of us that I had.

"Hailey's school called me yesterday. Asked me to come in for a parent/teacher conference today."

"That's pretty normal, right?" I watched her carefully. She was tense and buying wine in quantities I hadn't seen since she found a leg on her porch.

"Not with a one-day notice." She pulled out the wine, throwing the two whites in the fridge to chill as she opened the red and poured us both a glass.

Wow. That must have been some parent/teacher conference.

I took a sip as I waited for her to continue.

"Turns out, Hailey's been listening to Gran and Aunt Helen talk about *The Incident* and has been telling people at school. They had to report it to social services. Who were also there. To talk to me about my body part problems." She downed half the glass.

Wine came flying out of my mouth, spraying the white marble counter in front of me. I could just picture Lark, sitting there with the principal and two people from Social Services trying to explain why she had received body parts on her doorstep. Lark didn't look like she thought it was funny, but she was just too close to it. It absolutely was that funny.

"They then had to call Benny to come down to the school and give them the report in person." Lark slumped into one of my counter seats as she took another drink from her glass, draining the rest in one gulp. "They pulled the Chief of Police down to collaborate my story, Jen."

Watching her as I finished wiping down the counter, I sipped again from the glass she refilled, making sure it stayed in this time.

"Do you know what the first thing Benny asked me was? The *first thing*, Jen?"

"I have no idea." I completely had an idea. I just wanted to make her say it.

"'When's Brecken going to join the force, Lark? Aren't you going to make him move here?'" She mimicked our Chief of Police's voice badly, but it didn't matter. I was laughing too hard. "Why can't everyone just butt out of our relationship? Or understand that we are taking it slow. Slow. I will not be whored out so that Barrow Bay can get a new Chief."

"I don't know if taking a job counts as payment. It isn't really whoring… More of an unconventional benefit," I argued.

"*No*. I'm *not* an unconventional benefit." Lark glared, backing up her words.

"No. You're right. Stand up for your rights. Burn your bras. Feminists unite," I mocked. She was completely right, but I had made a promise to our Chief's wife, Alice.

"Whoa. I like my bras. Do you know how much I have to pay for good bras that hold up for riding? Judges don't like to see jiggling. Anywhere. It takes money to strap these babies down." Lark was a dressage trainer, and she was frequently gone at horse shows where she…

did something on horses. She mentioned pretty horse dancing a lot, so there was maybe music, too. I knew there were levels. She mentioned those a lot, as well.

"You're a size B at the most. You don't know what true jiggle is."

"And yet I still spend a fortune. Men have it so much easier."

"Pink tax." It was expensive to be a woman. Way more expensive than being a man.

"No kidding. Do you know how much jockstraps are? Not eighty bucks, I'll tell you that."

"So, no bra burning. Still, maybe you might… *push* him into thinking about Barrow Bay. Just a little." I looked through the empty grocery bag to hide my face.

"Not you, too. Who got to you?"

Oops. I had told Alice I was bad at this.

"Alice. She was complaining about how much she wants Benny to retire. There were tears, Lark. Tears. And I like Brecken. He would be perfect." Benny had been the Chief here in Barrow Bay for decades. Alice, his purple-haired impish wife, had big plans for what they were going to do when he retired. Which would be as soon as he found a replacement. The only thing standing in their way was Lark's admittedly logical fear of commitment and Brecken's wish to not leave his sister. All great points, but here, in Barrow Bay, he had been chosen, and they would do anything to make it so.

"I'm not pushing. Or luring. Or convincing. Or bribing. None of it. We are taking it slow and I'm happy." Lark crossed her arms, her eyes narrowed and staring into the distance. Now that I thought about it, she might have been glaring at her Gran's Tea House.

"I know. You glow every time you get a message. It's slightly annoying." She looked over at me and there it was: pity. The same expression I saw on all my city friends faces, too. It wasn't like I avoided love. I wanted marriage and children and the whole picture. I just liked financial security, too. Or, if I was to be completely honest, more. If it was a toss-up between love or financial security, I knew which one would win.

Although, I was starting to think maybe I had prioritized the wrong one. My security hadn't ended up being as secure as I'd expected.

"How's online dating going?" she asked, giving me a sympathetic look.

"Do you see any dates?" I replied.

"Well, since bringing your best friend on dates is awkward, I didn't really think that was an indicator."

"I've been working." Not knowing if I would have a business anymore had been a big motivator. I had a tidy nest egg. My house was paid off. I had enough money to survive my current business going under, even as I fought tooth and nail to keep it going. Eventually, people would trust me again. It was not like I was involved in the crime. Just the oblivious partner who didn't catch on to the corruption until it was too late. Because that was a great reason to convince people to let me help them with their business.

But... what if no one did? What if people couldn't get over my partner being a crook, and that carried over to me by association? What if I ran out of money? What if I got sick?

My chest hurt. I needed more money in my savings. Just in case.

"What about after working?" Lark's voice interrupted my anxiety cycle.

I took a longer sip of wine as I turned my attention back to her. And my lack of dating life. I was failing personally and professionally. I was heading into pathetic.

"I sleep. Then work some more." Good thing, too. Since the feds showed up again today. I could already guess I was going to get more phone calls tomorrow. Bye-bye to that last thirty percent.

"You need to stop. Breathe. Get food." She gestured to my cabinets. Which were bare. Again. "Maybe pick up a cool habit like drinking coffee."

I laughed. Lark and her addiction. "Your coffee obsession is disturbing."

"Someone not liking coffee is disturbing."

My phone pinged that I was getting a text. Shaking my head at her silliness, I took it out of my pocket and looked. It was Henry. That wasn't too surprising, considering the FBI agent at my door. I hadn't talked with him much since the investigation started. I… couldn't. I was too hurt that he had done this, letting me down in such a manner. He knew I needed financial security, that it was everything to me. How could he have done this to our company?

Before the scandal, Henry lived in the city, and until this year, had taken most of the face-to-face meetings. We previously had quite a clientele of businesses that didn't want to pay for a full time CPA, but still wanted the professional knowledge, even if the price tag was hefty. Hiring us, and paying only when needed was still cheaper than hiring someone with our level of knowledge. We catered to them by providing the service at a reduced cost based on need. It had been a thriving business, and we were thinking about taking on two new CPAs. Until the investigation, that is.

Henry: *We need to talk. I want to explain everything. Can you meet me at the resort tomorrow? 9 am?*

I was confused. I should've expected him to want to talk, but for him to come to Barrow Bay? Henry never left the city. I was pretty sure he considered Sausalito an exotic locale. He had never met me here, not in the six years I worked with him. He had, after my mother died, tried to convince me to move back to the city, but I'd come to love it here.

Barrow Bay was my comfort zone. Consisting of Main Street, the resort, and about 1,000 stubborn people who made it work, give or take a few, it was tight-knit enough that everyone knew everyone, but the resort kept it in touch with culture. Well, the culture that appealed to the older generations, at least.

My mother had lived here when fishing was something people could make money doing without a major rig. Then she left to marry my dad. Big mistake. Twenty-five years later, she returned to Barrow Bay broke and broken. My father had been a con artist hiding behind the title of a salesperson. Always looking for a quick buck and an even quicker return. Every dollar he earned went back out into some new investment that was going to make us all rich. The funny thing, eventually it paid off. He got rich. Then he got rid of us. My mother was good enough for the small time, but he needed a trophy wife to show around his new club. We were disposable. So, she came back to her home town, while I graduated from high school a year early and went to college.

Six years later, I had a B.S. in accounting, an MBA, and an ailing mother. That was when Henry stepped in. I had worked with him when he mentored some of our classes. He'd been impressed and when he heard of my situation, he had a solution. I went home with a good job, one that could pay the medical bills and give my mother the help she needed. But even the best medical care couldn't save someone who didn't want to be saved.

Me: *I have a meeting. Can we do 10 am?*

I waited for his answer. It took longer than usual, but maybe he was doing something at the same time.

Henry: *I can make that work. 10 am.*

Me: *Great. Where do you want to meet?*

Henry: *Room 304*

Huh. Interesting.

Me: *Ok. See you then.*

"Lark? Have you ever stayed at the hotel before?"

"Yeah, before I moved here. Blake hated staying with Gran." Lark made the same face she always did when she mentioned her ex-husband. A pained expression that was equal parts disgust and, well, more disgust.

"Aren't the lower end numbers suites?" I frowned at the phone. "Like the first five rooms in the resort on each floor?"

"I think so. We never stayed in them, but Mom and Dad did a few times. Why?" She walked closer to me so she could peek over my shoulder.

"Henry is in town. Staying at the hotel in room 304."

"Henry? As in your business partner? I thought he refused to travel out here."

"So did I."

"Wonder what he wants. Did it have anything to do with the Wolverine?" Lark asked, looking me in the eye so I couldn't lie.

"I'm going to guess so. Coincidences don't happen like that very often." I sighed. "Also, Wolverine? Is that what we are going with?"

"Agent Ass Hat and Agent Unimportant got voted too long. Nic's too personal, and I refuse to call him Satan without hooves and horns to go with it. Wolverine it is."

Fabulous. She had just nicknamed my secret crush with my favorite superhero's name. This had better not be a sign.

CHAPTER 3

The next morning, I was surprised to not find more FBI agents at my door. I knew that things took a while, but TV had me conditioned to expect instantaneous results. Turn in the crime tip, next day the SEC or FBI would be swarming all over trying to find evidence. Even now that I knew it didn't work that way, I still expected to wake up to a warrant and a team of forensic accountants. Honestly, I was kind of excited to meet them this time. Forensic accounting sounded interesting, and I didn't get to talk to them last time because I'd been too busy yelling at Nic. I might have thrown a vase. And a book, one of the self-help books he pointed out the first day. Evidently, I had some trouble keeping my cool around him.

Or I was taking my anger and guilt out on him. No, no, I was going with it being his fault. It wasn't the most mature decision, but I couldn't stop my emotions from snapping, and it was easier to blame him for the reaction than face reality.

It turned out that I was big on deflecting blame when it came to my life imploding.

I contacted my lawyer before my nine am meeting to go over what to do and say and was now more prepared. After we went over everything, I also told him to start the paperwork to close the business. Just in case I couldn't turn it around. That was the hardest part of the call. I may have cried. Twice.

At nine-thirty, as soon as my call was over, I got ready to leave, slipping on my favorite shoes. They were simple black pumps with a red sole, but they were my first pair of Louboutins. The first truly expensive, frivolous thing I had bought for myself after my mother died and I paid off all her debts. I could do anything in these shoes. A quick touch-up on my makeup and I was ready to go, my blonde hair swept back into a neat ponytail, held together by hairspray, and my blue eyes accented by mascara. I was a professional. I was strong. I was… going to be late if I didn't leave now.

I pulled out in my sedan, one that I got extra cheap because evidently everyone hated blue that year, and headed for the short drive to the resort. I lived two blocks back from the south side of our downtown in a newer neighborhood, but it still didn't take me long to get to Main Street and turn north. Main Street was the center of our town, the place where most of the stores and businesses sold their wares. On the west side was a row of restaurants and bars that catered to tourists. In the middle used to be Tops, or Topped Off Coffee Pot, but it had recently closed. The town had been trying to find someone to take over the lease, hopefully staying the same as the coffee shop had been a big tourist attraction, but there hadn't been anyone interested yet. At least, there hadn't been anyone that the town approved of.

On the east side of the street were all the shops that didn't need an ocean view to sell their wares. Grocery, liquor store, antiques. If tourists would buy it, these stores would sell it. People who lived an hour away from any source of large industry had to be resourceful. And willing to do whatever it took to make a dollar. I would know. I did the taxes for a few of the stores in my free time.

Passing the shops, I continued north until the road changed from cheap asphalt to expensive pavement, a sign that travelers had entered a different world. As always, I held my breath as the resort came into view. The resort was a four-story palace, complete with large twisting staircases and white sand pillars. I loved it. Everyone loved it. Hell, even Lark, with her hatred of anything built after the 1950s, loved it. I had always wanted to stay there, even for one night, but never justified the expense.

I pulled into a parking spot and turned off my car, breathing through my mouth to try to relieve the tightness in my chest. My anxiety was like a clamp on my heart, but I pushed it down. I didn't have the option of letting it win. I had to make money. To support myself. To get out of this car and be the powerful business partner I pretended to be. Not the scared, anxiety-ridden, stress ball that I really was. In a lot of things my anxiety would win. Leaving town. Dating. I would back down, run away, escape. But not business. Financial security was everything.

One last breath and I got out.

And stopped dead in my tracks.

"Wolverine?" *Shit.* I didn't mean to call him that. He loved it, though. His surprise turned into a huge smirk, and he shifted his body into an arrogant car lean. The stupid romantic in me appreciated the aesthetic of it. He was perfectly framed in the light, and somehow his black suit didn't blend in against the black SUV that I hoped was his. Wait, he was driving an SUV?

"Are you serious? You actually drive an SUV?" That made him stand up and lose his grin. In fact, his face took on a slightly hurt expression as he looked over his ride.

Oops.

"What? It's a great car. I can get anywhere in this. Even in snow."

"Well, I'm *so* glad that you are *so* prepared. Too bad we're on the coast of California, though. I don't know if it has ever snowed in Barrow Bay. But good for you to be prepared." Hmm, I was a little defensive today. I should rethink that. Being nice to the federal agents investigating your company was a much better idea. Plus, I was kind of impressed he liked to be ready for anything. Even snow that was unlikely. I did, too. Maybe I could turn over a new leaf in relation to dealing with Nic. Maybe even stop calling him Satan. It could happen.

His glare lingered for a second before his cocky grin returned. He had a zinger.

I braced myself.

"I like to *always* be prepared." He waggled his dark brows and fake leered.

Double entendres and an FBI badge. How talented. Either way, I was unmoved. Okay, that was a lie, but I was pretending to be. Thinking about kissing the FBI agent who was here to investigate my company would be bad. Again.

"You have been skating off your good looks for too long, haven't you?" So much for being nice. Who was I kidding? I enjoyed fighting him too much to be nice. His unpolished reactions were so much better than his flirting. More real.

"What?" His mouth dropped open as I walked closer.

"You. You have been skating by, using your good looks and—" I tapped my chin as I pretended to think. "—*charm* to get by. It's made your comebacks rusty. You should have more people in your life that challenge you." I stopped and, like I'd seen Dorothy, the owner of the resort, do when she was angry, I looked him up and down. "Then you might not have to depend on whoring yourself out for information."

Hah. That was a good one. And I was super glad for Lark's complaints last night. I would have never come up with the insult if I hadn't been listening to her.

His mouth worked as he tried to process me calling him an information-whore. I felt kind of bad. He hadn't actually been mean or even that rude this time. Just cocky. Manipulative. Arrogant. My ex-boyfriend had been like that. Confident and the center of his world. I didn't need that again. Ever.

I sighed. What a mess.

"Well, I have a meeting, so I'm going to have to leave now. Have a nice day." I rushed past him, careful not to touch him in any way. Touching would be bad. He was hot, and I was not prepared for hormone overload. I was not good at telling myself no. I always ate dessert, too. That was how my butt got to be this size. And he was a pumpkin pie, wrapped in chocolate cake, covered in fudge. Probably tasted good going down but would make me sick after.

"Where are you going? Who are you meeting?" Nicholas recovered from his shock to trail after me.

"Don't you have somewhere to be? People to torment? Warrants to serve? Lives to ruin?"

"I like to think of my job as *saving* lives." He fell into step beside me.

He had a point. I might've overplayed that last one.

"Have you?" I asked, unable to stop myself from being curious.

"Saved a life?" He smirked, looking over to see how interested I was in his life-saving actions.

Sigh. That smirk was getting old. And I was a little too interested.

"Never mind. I don't want to know. I can see your ego getting bigger from here."

"My ego is a healthy reaction to talent." He settled back into stride, scanning the hotel as we approached.

"I get the car now. You need room for your ego to ride shotgun."

"You seem very interested in my car."

"SUV," I corrected. Man. The class know-it-all tone really came out in that one. I had outgrown the pigtails, but not the need to be the most correct.

"*You* called it a car."

"It's an SUV. You should have corrected me, not echoed the wrong terminology." Oh god. I was getting anal. I was so awkward. Also, I couldn't believe I thought the word 'anal' while around him. Bad thoughts. Bad. Would he understand if I asked him not to talk while I got my thoughts back from the gutter? "Anyway. I'm late. Have a nice day." Escape, stage left. Or in this case, stage right since that was where the elevators were.

"Maybe I'll walk you in." He kept pace with me, shooting me another grin.

"Do I have another option?"

"Not really."

Fabulous. I turned and walked away, trying to ignore the shadow behind me. I could do it. I could just pretend he's not there. It was all good.

"So, do your customers usually come to see you? I would have thought you would travel to them. Shouldn't that be part of the service?"

"It is," I snapped. *Shit.* Ignoring him again.

"So then, who are we going to meet?"

"No one." Why did my mouth keep opening?

"You look awfully pretty to be meeting no one." He leaned back as we hesitated for the front doors to open, giving me a look over.

Bastard. "Maybe I'm going on a date."

"At 10 am? On a Tuesday?" He tsked. "He can't have a job then. Not good enough for you."

Good enough...? No. Ignoring. But did he think about what guys I should date? And he had high expectations? *Focus.*

"I will take your advice into consideration." He didn't know it, but that was my version of the F word. The one I used on CEOs when they thought they understood finance better than I did. I remembered a time when I was impressed with titles. When I thought CEOs were business geniuses, devious chess players, thinking five moves ahead. Giants among men. Before I found out that CEOs were people. And that what got them to the top of their company was hard work, connections, and having little life outside of work. Business genius could be hired. I proved that.

I walked through the resort lobby with angry clicks. Halfway through the beautiful lobby, the sound of my heels on the marble floors soothed me. Centered me. I was in control. People who wore these shoes were always in control. The elevator doors opened to let some guests off and I hurried in, hoping Agent Nosy-Pants wouldn't follow. No luck. He snuck in right as the door closed. He even did the sexy side slip-thru, sneaking past the closing doors like I had seen in the movies, his signature smirk telling me he was only letting me think I might escape him.

No. That was not sexy. I was in control. Me. Not my hormones. Nope.

"So, can I know where we're going yet?"

Fine. Why not?

"To see Henry."

"Your business partner?"

"Yes."

"Why?" he asked, leaning on the wall, one leg bent against it.

It was still sexy, but now I couldn't help but feel bad for the poor people who were going to have to clean the shoe print off the shiny sides.

"Can you sound any less suspicious?" I snapped.

"No." He thought for a second. "No, I really can't."

I had the sudden inclination to hit my head on the elevator doors. Or his. I let myself enjoy that image for a while before reminding myself that assault was bad, and assaulting a federal agent was worse.

"I don't know," I finally answered, focusing my gaze on the door and not the man I had just confessed to.

"You don't know why I can't be less suspicious? Well, your partner—"

"Hush." I looked around at the empty elevator to confirm it was empty. Because I was that paranoid. "Whatever you *think* you may have, nothing has been confirmed." Well, convicted. Innocent until proven guilty, right? "Please don't go throwing around accusations." That got me another look of pity. Two in one week. I was on a roll. "And I was answering your question. I don't know why I'm here. He texted last night and asked me."

"Really." His face closed off. Well, at least it wasn't pity. The elevator dinged, and the doors opened. I rushed off, orienting myself quickly to find the room I wanted. I checked my phone. 10:10. I was late. Henry was going to be pissed.

310… 308… 306… there. 304. I found it, my shadow still right behind me.

Bang.

I jumped and looked down at my hands. I hadn't knocked yet.

Wait. That wasn't me. What was that sound?

Suddenly I was flying toward the wall, an arm around my waist anchoring me to the side. Nicholas's body was between me and the hall and he had his phone out, dialing.

"John. Shots fired. Room 304."

Shots? As in 'bang, bang'? As in a gun? No. There was only one bang. It couldn't be a gun.

Oh my god. *Shots fired.*

"Henry." I had to get to him. I didn't care if he was a criminal. He was my friend. He had to be okay. I struggled to get out of Nicholas's arms, but he was too strong. "Henry!"

Soon I registered Nicholas's voice. "Easy. Easy, gorgeous. I need you to stop struggling."

I got a hold of my panic, his rhythmic rubbing of my arms easing me back from my blind terror enough to look at him.

"Henry," I whispered. He seemed to understand my plea.

"If you promise to stay here, I will go check on him. But I need you to not do anything stupid."

"I never do anything stupid." My response was automatic, but less than honest.

I was completely going to follow him in. For Henry, I was exactly that stupid. He looked at my face and seemed to come to that conclusion, too.

Damn it.

"We have to go help him," I pleaded.

"Sure. If you swear to Excel that you will stay here," he replied.

Excel? The computer program? I was so confused.

"Fine. Whatever. Go help him," I lied. I was absolutely following. This time he believed me. He turned, pulling out a gun from somewhere and I watched in silence.

Maybe I *wouldn't* follow. I didn't do guns.

I tapped the wall as I thought.

Nope. Henry was in there. I was following. Maybe I could help Henry while Nic got the bad guy.

Nicholas held the gun still as he listened for a second before knocking. "This is the FBI, open the door!"

We both waited for a second, straining to hear any sound. Suddenly, Nic backed up and kicked the door, his foot hitting right next to the lock. The door gave, swinging open and he cautiously scanned the room as he entered.

Okay. I could do this. I could go help Henry. I took a step towards the room.

But it might be dangerous. I hesitated.

Something clanged. Was the shooter still in the room?

Henry. *Nicholas!*

Debate over, I rushed over to the door as a black blur ran out, shoving me aside into the door jamb as it fled.

"Stop!" Nic followed, his gun moving in search for the blur, but it was gone. He looked around confused.

"Stairs." Ouch. I had hit my arm hard. I rubbed it, hoping that would relieve the pain. Nic looked at me in confusion. "The stairwell is around the corner. He must have gone down." I pointed.

He nodded. "Don't go in there. It's a crime scene." Then he was gone, too.

Crime scene. No paramedics.

I pulled myself up, preparing to confirm my suspicions, pain swelling in my chest and threatening to take over.

I turned.

I was right.

Henry was dead.

CHAPTER 4

I was left with the body.

Umm. What should I do now? My only instinct was to call the cops and I'm pretty sure Nic had already done that. I turned and glanced at Henry again before I thought about it.

Shit. Stupid idea.

I turned halfway back around before I hesitated. Someone had killed him. Shot him while I was outside. What if I knew something? No. That was stupid. But he said he needed to talk to me. To explain. What if he wanted to tell me something that got him killed? I peeked.

Henry was face down in the middle of the suite, a red liquid pooling underneath him. Blood. Oh god. I took a deep breath and tried to separate myself from my emotions.

His hands were face down on the ground above his head. I imagined he was probably holding them up when the killer fired. I tore my eyes away, searching the room for anything out of place. There were bags sitting atop the bed on the far side of the room with items thrown around like they had been searched. The killer could have done it, but Henry wasn't a neat freak like me. What could the killer have been looking for? I took a step toward it before I stopped again. Nope. Not going near the body. Henry. Henry's body.

Oh my god.

Henry was dead. My anxiety rose up and buried me. At one point I was standing, and the next, I was sitting down in the doorway, the frame digging into my spine. Breathing. Okay, gasping for air. Where did it all go? Air couldn't disappear. It had to still be around me. All I needed to do was breathe it in. Why was I struggling with it?

"Jen?" John knelt in front of me, his tan hand contrasting sharply against my arm's paleness. A Hispanic man in his forties, John had come to Barrow Bay a few years ago. As he put it, he retired from the streets of LA to do what he enjoyed—being the town detective. "Are you okay?"

"He's dead," I whimpered, my head buried in my hands.

"Nicholas? Because I expected a few more days until you tried to kill him this time around."

What?

My head swung up. Oh. It was a joke. Distract the witness out of their shock. Good idea.

"You think I could take out an FBI agent?" He was good at this. I was thoroughly distracted. And enjoying the image of me smacking Nic around. Evidently, I had a vicious streak.

"When you found out why he was here? Absolutely." He smiled at me and I returned it. The thought of little five-foot-eight me taking on giant six-foot-six Nic and winning made me snort.

"Why *is* he here?" I asked, curious to know what John had privy to.

"I'll let him tell you. That way you can be mad at him. And only him. Remember that you love me. And my wife. You and Judy are great friends. You wouldn't want her to be husbandless, right?"

"Overly dramatic."

"Everyone's a critic." John leaned closer to let an officer by. That was when I noticed that we were surrounded.

Wow. When I freaked, I freaked.

"What do I do now?" I asked, my strength sagging as my amusement faded.

"We figure out why Henry wanted to talk to you," Nicholas's voice interrupted. John and I both turned to look at him as he walked up the hallway.

"He looks mad," I whispered, only to blush when I realized Nic overheard.

"Yep," John deadpanned, not showing his delight at my unintentional cheek.

"He isn't sexy when mad." I might still be in shock.
"Is anyone?"

"I don't know. They always say that in the movies," I answered honestly.

"Only to the girls. Maybe it's a girl thing," John joked, shifting his weight as he knelt. That had to be uncomfortable.

"Could be," I conceded, risking a peek at Nic.

Nic just glared at both of us. "You two done? Or is there more to your comedy routine?"

"I don't know. Maybe we should analyze this some more. We might be onto a breakthrough for relations between the sexes. Maybe write a book. TV appearances." I smiled innocently at Nic, trying to hide how much teasing him made me feel better. Well, less like I was going to cry at any moment.

"Okay. I'm splitting you two up. John, can you go see where the coroner is?"

"The Bahamas." That made Nic stop and glance at him.

"Excuse me?"

"Our coroner is in the Bahamas. We have to call the county coroner," John clarified.

"When are we going to admit that he's not coming back?" I asked. He'd been gone for three months now. I figured we could officially say he had island fever.

"When we find the right fit," John admitted.

Well, at least they were honest. That was how this town worked. When a position came open, the powers that be looked for the right replacement. Most recently, Brecken for Chief. Lark was underestimating their commitment. I was looking forward to the town's next move.

Nic gave us both a look that clearly communicated he thought we were crazy.

"Whatever. Can you check on the county coroner?" he asked, through clenched teeth.

I didn't think he liked our responses. I got it. We didn't respond like normal people. Flippant and sarcastic was how we survived in this town. Also, probably why we had to search for the right fit.

"Nope," John answered, giving me a small wink.

Nic's eyes closed for a second before he took a deep breath and turned to John again. "Why?"

"He's downstairs. Happened to be in town, so he wasn't that far behind me."

Counting. I was pretty sure that's why Nic's mouth was moving. He was counting.

"Great." He turned and looked around. "Where can we interview Jennifer?"

"Jen," I snapped.

His chest heaved with the strength of his sigh. He was lying to himself. He was too dramatic to be Wolverine. Maybe Cyclops would work, though. Cyclops was always more dramatic.

Oh my gosh. I had been hanging around Lark too long. Her comic book movie obsession had rubbed off.

"Interview room?" Nic ignored my comment and continued to address John.

"Dorothy is working on getting us the room next door. Zach?" John called out to another officer in uniform. "Did you have a chance to get the key card yet?"

"Yeah, right here." Zach held up a key card and Nic took it with an exasperated look.

"He's not Captain America," I commented to John, who held back a snort.

"Again with the Captain America." Nic rolled his eyes and walked to the other door, using the key to open it. "Your room, milady."

Yep. Definitely not a grumpy anti-hero with a heart of gold like Wolverine. Just grumpy.

I walked into the suite. It was just like Henry's only in reverse. Another wave of pain hit me. Henry was gone. What would I do next? Should I call his clients and tell them? I wasn't even completely sure who his clients were. His son had been helping him more and more over the past few years and I had gotten busier with my own. Not that I had cared. I had enough business on my own.

Oh, god. I would have to contact his son.

"Frank. I need to call Frank." I stood to grab my phone from my purse, but Nic stopped me.

"Frank Boyd? Henry's son?"

"Yes. He needs to know…" Nic was blocking me, so I turned and walked over to the window. I watched two cars leave, a red sedan and a blue truck, passing through the police perimeter. I watched quietly as their tail lights disappeared down the road.

"Jen?" Nic asked from behind me. "Can you go over what brought you here today?" His voice was gentle. It was strange. A soft Nic. I shook off the thought, focusing on how I could help them with the investigation.

"Henry texted me out of the blue last night. Said we needed to talk. Gave me the time and place. He wanted to meet me at nine, but I had a call this morning, so I had to push it back." I rubbed my arms as that thought sunk in. Would he still be alive if I had been here at nine? Could I have saved him? If I'd cancelled that phone call?

"Can I see the text messages?"

"Yes! Yes, it's in my purse." I pointed and he went to grab it for me. Searching through it, I found my phone, unlocked it and pulled up the conversation. I could do this. I could help solve his murder. That was an action. A plan. Well, an action that might lead to a plan.

"And this is it? Have you guys communicated recently other than this?"

"No. Not since..." I trailed off and faced the window again. Could my actions have caused this? Was it a client trying to keep Henry from talking? It seemed ridiculous, but people had killed for less.

"Not since the warrants were served," he concluded.

"Yes. I... I've had trouble working with him since I found the documents," I admitted. It wasn't like he didn't know.

"How did you get Tony's account? From my understanding, he had been a long-time client of Henry's."

"Henry was thinking about retiring, so he was starting to shift more demanding customers to me." I got tired of talking to the window, so I walked over to the table and sat, with Nic following me. He took the chair across from me and I focused on the table. I was ready to tell him everything. "We were looking at hiring two new people, one to replace Henry and one to expand the business."

"When was he planning on retiring?"

"A year? Maybe two? We hadn't set a date. We were too busy to do more than mention it and say we needed to hire someone. Henry handled all of that."

"What about his son? He has a degree in business."

"Didn't pass the test to be a CPA. We do more than just taxes and bookkeeping. He needed to have his license to meet all our clients' needs. I know Henry used him as needed for some of the more routine stuff, but he was always supervised." I tried to keep my tone even, but Nic noticed the grimace.

"You don't like him," he commented.

"I don't hate him."

"I thought you liked everyone. Pretty sure I had a tall, skinny girl yelling that at me last night."

I smiled at the memory. It felt weird with what just happened, but I couldn't hold it back. That was why I loved this town. No matter how down I was, it always made me laugh. "He isn't a bad guy. I don't dislike him. I just… don't like him. I disliked working with him when we worked together. He… wasn't good at his job." That was probably an overshare, but maybe it would be helpful.

"Are there any other people that work for your business occasionally?"

"Henry had a tax specialist who would help out during tax season, but I don't know her name. He took care of it. As far as I know, there wasn't any bad blood. They wouldn't want to kill him. I have a few months before tax season, so I haven't contacted them yet."

"You weren't very active in the running of the business for a partner."

"I work seventy to eighty hours a week. I get my job done and I keep my clients happy. That is my job. Making it run is Henry's." He had been the foundation of the company, until three weeks ago. Since then I had been doing everything, and this conversation was proving to me how many things I probably had missed. Nic was right. I should've known all of these specifics to the answers if I had been running the business for three weeks. I had been too busy fielding customers calls, trying to stop them from withdrawing their accounts. I wiped away a tear from the corner of my eye. I hadn't noticed when my eyesight went blurry, but had felt the wetness on my cheek.

"What will you do now?"

"I don't know." It came out as a whisper, like I was afraid to say the truth too loudly. I thought about it, tracing a line in the table absently, before admitting the hard truth. "Probably shut it down. Start my own business with any clients that will follow."

He studied me for a minute, before leaning back, his eyes still watching my face intently.

"Tony Harris was charged three days ago. As will Dan Ellson. Soon."

It was official. We had aided in a crime. Well, the company had. *Henry* had. Two crimes, since I recognized Dan Ellson as another of Henry's clients, although not one as big as Tony or the Harris corporate accounts. My head dropped into my hands as I dealt with the reality. Even though I knew it was coming, hearing it hurt. No. It didn't hurt anymore. Because it couldn't. I had nothing left to feel.

Wait. "Do you think Tony or Dan killed Henry because they thought he turned them in?" That made sense. I relaxed. This would be straightforward. Nic would find the murderer, either Tony or Dan and I could move—

"No. Henry's accounts were frozen as well. He was facing criminal charges too."

"Why wasn't I told?" I asked quietly. I was too numb to be angry. I was too numb to be anything.

"We wanted to know what you knew. I didn't know you submitted the tip until last night." He sighed. "Although, I should've guessed quicker. You were always a piece that didn't fit into the story." He looked away for a second before looking back at me, more pity in his eyes. "I don't know why Henry didn't tell you."

"Why would anyone kill Henry?"

"I don't know," he admitted, leaning back in his chair. "But we will find out."

I nodded, unsure what I was supposed to say to that.

"What do you need to help?" Maybe he could give me a plan.

"Access to your records."

I nodded absently. Yeah, I should have seen that coming. "No." My voice was firm, but calm, a first in my history of dealing with Nic. Usually I lost my control over my good sense.

He looked up in question. "No?"

"Client protection. You still need a warrant." Although, for the first time, I really did wish I could do it. For Henry. Then again, it might make everything worse. I didn't know if I could take another client being dirty. No, there was no way any of my clients were dirty. Then again, there had been a time I would've said that about Henry's, too.

His lips pressed together, but he didn't say anything. The twitch in his lips made me think that he might be impressed by my defiance and hiding it. I definitely sensed approval even though that made no sense. I was refusing to make his life easier.

"Anything else?" I asked, tired and still unsure of what to do next. I was out of helpful information. I had to think.

"Not right now. We'll be in touch."

"Right." My mind drifted away from the interview.

Step One: contact my clients. Tell them… I didn't know what to tell them.

"Do you want one of the officers to drive you home?" Nic's voice interrupted my thoughts.

"No. I'm fine." I stood, pulling myself up to my full height plus the two inches from my heels. "I'm fine," I repeated. I could do this. I had my heels.

He sat there assessing me for a second before nodding. His hand drifted toward me for a second before dropping back to his side as he turned away.

"Bye, Cyclops," I told his back as I walked out.

"Hey. I thought we decided I was Wolverine. Cyclops is too whiny," he called out from behind me.

"Yep." I walked out before he could say anything else. John was in the hall coordinating people. "You need anything?" I asked him. Shouldn't he have been in the interview with us?

"No. I'll get it from Nic later." He smiled. "You two seemed... chummy."

"No. You already got your chief-in-waiting. Go bother Lark," I said, throwing her under the bus with a look that should tell him not to mess with me. I was not Lark. I would not put up with them messing with me like they did her.

He smiled.

I needed to give Lark more sympathy. Something was up, and I had a feeling I was involved this time. That was not a good smile.

"You know... the resort is hiring." He paused dramatically.

I stared, not buying whatever he was selling. "So?"

"And they need a security expert. Someone who can handle high status clientele and security issues."

Oh. My. God.

"No," I hissed. "You do not just start kidnapping any man who comes to town. No. Nic goes back to wherever he came from."

"Why am I going back? And here I was starting to think we were getting along."

I spun around.

"Will you stop doing that?" This was the second time he had walked into a conversation. My nerves couldn't handle it.

"I must say, I'm intrigued by this kidnapping idea. Is it just you or is the whole town in on it?"

I... He... I had nothing. I just stared at him with my mouth hanging open.

"I'm out. Done. Finished. Played out. Washed up—"

"How long can she go like this?" Nic asked John, who shrugged, watching me with amusement.

"—wiped out, drained, exhausted."

"She's one of those people that got a perfect score on the vocab part of the SATs, didn't she?" Nic commented, as he shook his head.

"Looks that way," John replied, smiling at my frustration.

"Oh." I turned and stomped away, only to stop and spin around, walking over to Nic and getting in his face. "I warned you. When everything's out of control and you wonder how you ended up where you did, look back at this moment and realize *I told you*." With that, I turned and left, my heels echoing down the hall. Storming out in heels was the best. They gave you a click that vibrated throughout the hall, announcing my anger to everyone. That was the sign of great shoes.

They let everyone know when not to mess with me.

CHAPTER 5

I didn't make it out of the hotel before it hit me
again. My partner was dead. My mentor. The face
of our business. I didn't want to move. I didn't want
to live in the city. I didn't want to be Henry. That led to
one conclusion.

I was out of a job.

Well, that wasn't quite correct. I was going to *give
up* my business. Consciously. On purpose. No *maybe*.
No *just in case*. It was done.

I needed to sit down.

Finding a pale tan leather couch in the corner of the
lobby, I collapsed into it, trying to figure out where to
go from here.

I need a plan. Yes. A plan. What do I do now?

Step One: I needed to do what I should have done
two months ago. Shut down the business. Tell my clients
what was happening and see if they wanted to stay with
me alone. Find someone to take the remaining few
clients of Henry's and any others that had concerns. It
was going to hurt, but that was the correct thing to do.
Right? Or should I wait until the investigation was over?
Maybe that wouldn't be Step One. Putting a pin in that.

Step Two: I took a deep breath… tell Charlotte and Frank what happened. I would have to remote into Henry's computer to get their contact information. Or would the cops do that, too? I didn't know. I should've asked John before I left.

Step Three…

"Hello."

I looked up at the child in front of me. He looked to be about the same age as Lark's daughter, maybe seven or eight at the oldest. His blond hair needed a haircut as it drifted into his eyes, which were blue as they peeked through and a slight smile on his face.

"Hello. Where's your parents?" I asked, putting aside my bad planning.

"My daddy is a bad man," he told me, his voice solemn and quiet.

"My daddy is a bad man, too." Now my surrogate father was as well. I may not have escaped the damage my father did as well as I thought. "What did your daddy do?" I patted the empty space on the couch next to me.

"He hit my mommy. But my uncle made him go away."

What do you say to that? And why would he share this with me? A total stranger?

"Your uncle sounds like a good guy," I offered.

"He is, but we hate his job." His little head bobbed up and down, like I imagined he had seen the adult do when they said it. Little mockingbirds.

"We?" I asked.

"My mom and my grandparents."

"Okay." I had no idea where this was going.

"We're coming here to see if we like it."

"Barrow Bay?" I was shocked. Very few people moved here under the age of 65. 'Sleepy little town' was an understatement.

"Yep. Grandma says that it has attractive people."

Well, they might be disappointed once they got here, if that's what they were looking for.

"Attractive people?" I asked, hoping maybe he had heard wrong.

"He means attractive prospects," a voice interrupted. I looked up at a tall woman with blonde hair and blue eyes that matched the little boy next to me, albeit more frazzled and panicked. "I'm so sorry. I thought he was right next to me and then he was gone."

"No worries. We were just talking." I smiled up at her, letting her know it wasn't a big deal. I had lost Hailey, Lark's daughter, enough times, even for just a few seconds, to know what she felt like right now. Kids were fast.

"Her daddy is bad like mine," he told her.

I blushed and looked away. Funny how it had been comfortable to tell a little child, but telling an adult was embarrassing. "He wasn't that bad. Just... Well, I—"

"It's okay. I understand," she answered quickly. "I'm Julia."

"Jen."

"I'm Logan," Logan interrupted. "Wanna see my car collection?"

"He collects toy cars with his uncle," Julia clarified.

"That's so cool, but I need to get going. I have to…"
My throat closed. I didn't know what to tell a kid.
Definitely not that I needed to tell my partner's ex-wife
that he had been murdered that morning. "…work."

"You look sad. Does your work make you sad?"
Logan asked, patting my hand.

It was so cute I almost burst into tears, the ones I'd
been holding back with all my strength.

"No. I love my work. It's…" All I do. My life. The
reason I didn't have a boyfriend. The reason I stress-
shopped. Funny how none of those reasons were
positive. "…it's fun."

"What do you do?"

"I play with numbers all day."

"That doesn't sound fun."

Truth. It really didn't. But it was. There was a time
that I couldn't wait to wake up and get to my computer.

"It is. I love it." Or, at least, I used to. When did I
stop loving it?

"You sure?"

I laughed at the question. It was sad, but still a
laugh. "What do you do?"

"I'm too young to have a job. I go to school."

"Do you like school?"

"I like my friends."

"But some parts of school aren't fun, right?"

"I guess."

"Work's like that. No matter how much you love
your job, there will be parts of it you won't like."

He narrowed his eyes while he thought about that. "Okay. I guess so."

"Jen. Julia. I'm so glad the two of you have met." Dorothy Watts, the owner of the resort and one of the town's gossip queens, rushed over. Dorothy was in her early eighties, with hair that was too pure white for her to not have been someone who grayed early. She was also so graceful and stately that I was always a little jealous of her charisma. All a person had to do was look at her and they would be charmed by her welcoming smile. "Jen, darling. How are you?"

"I'm..." Numb? Lost? Without a plan? "Fine."

She reached in close and pulled me into a hug. "Do you need anything? Anything at all?"

"Not to be me." Not that it was a reasonable request.

"Well, maybe I could distract you? To be honest, I could use your help." She scanned my face. "If you're up to it?"

"What can I do for you?" I could get behind a distraction. My head was not a place I wanted to be in. The town's crazy plans sounded so much better. Mischief and hijinks were better than tears and depression. Denial worked for me.

"Can you show Julia around the town tomorrow?" Dorothy looked around at the people in the lobby before stepping closer. "I need it done quietly, though," she whispered.

"Avoid Lindsey. Got it."

"Who's Lindsey?" Julia asked.

"And Lark," Dorothy added.

"And Lark?" Wait. What was happening? This just got way more interesting. I had to give it to Dorothy. I asked for a distraction, and boy, did she deliver.

"Who's Lark?" Julia asked.

"No one, dear. No one." Dorothy patted Julia on the shoulder. "I want to make your vacation as fabulous as possible."

"Oh, no. You shouldn't do any more than you already are. Giving us a discount on the rooms is enough." Julia put her hand on Dorothy's in a polite denial.

"Nonsense. You need to get out. See the nightlife. Meet new people. See everything Barrow Bay has to offer."

Last I checked Barrow Bay didn't have a nightlife to offer, so I was a little confused on what she was requesting. "Dorothy—"

"Please, Jen. For me?" Dorothy blinked rapidly.

Did I see a tear forming? Alice had told them all my weakness. She had outed me. I knew this would happen. *Sigh.*

"Sure. Why not?" I could use it to delay my grief for a while. Plus, how long would it take? We had two blocks of Main Street. And the resort, which they had already seen. Maybe we could do lunch and it might take two hours. "How about I pick you guys up at eleven tomorrow?"

"You sure?" Julia asked, pulling Logan to her. "You seem to be going through something."

"Yes. Sure. It'll be fun. We can meet here at eleven," I told her. "See you then." I waved as they left the lobby, Logan already chatting about something and Julia listening.

"What's your schedule like tomorrow?" Dorothy asked, looking guilty.

I turned to face Dorothy, my eyes narrow and my arms crossed. "You want something more than me giving a tour?" My tone clearly suggested I wasn't happy. I was already doing a favor, I had things to do, alcohol to buy, tears to shed. I didn't know how much more denial was healthy.

"Yes." She glanced around and then pulled me further into the corner. "We need you for Operation Captain America."

"No."

"But you don't even—"

"My—" I couldn't say it. I took a deep breath and tried again. "No." Okay, less than stellar but it got the point across.

"Do you want to sit at home tomorrow?" Dorothy asked, her eyes soft. "You don't like to mourn. You threw yourself into work when your mother died. That isn't an option this time." She pulled me to her and quickly hugged me before moving back so she could look me in the eye. "Let me give you something else to work on."

Damn. She was good. I sighed, my shoulders slumping as I realized she was right. I didn't have anything to do but obsess about my feelings and how Henry's death would affect the business, and I really didn't want to do that.

"Why do I have a feeling Lark is involved?"

"Because you're smart."

"Why are we messing around in a relationship that's working just fine?" Granted, they were going slow, but still moving.

"Because Brecken needs a push. And Lark needs a shove."

"And?" Because that wasn't all of it.

"And—" She dragged out the word. "His parents agree he needs a new job."

"His parents agreed?" This officially had gotten out of control. Wildly and fabulously out of control. I took my issues back. I loved it. It would definitely be better than sitting at home crying.

"Yes. That's why they're here. With his sister." Dorothy gave me a big, fat smile.

And her son. Wow. I had seriously underestimated these ladies' commitment to matchmaking. And this town.

"Julia is Brecken's sister." I watched as Dorothy nodded. "And you don't want Lark to know." Another nod. "They are trying to decide if they want to move here." Look at that. Three for three. "This is going to be bad." But the laughter caused by the town plans was starting to overtake my grief.

"It will all work out. Just you wait." Dorothy smiled, clearly happy I had caved to her demands. I wouldn't have, but Lark looked so happy when she was around Brecken. Younger. Playful. My life was in shambles. Might as well make her life better. Maybe she could do the same when I started charging her for her taxes to make money for groceries.

"What do you want?" I asked, throwing myself into their plans completely.

"We need Lark away from her house tomorrow afternoon. Around two, if possible."

"And she won't be at work because…"

"Tomorrow's shots day." One day twice a year, all of the horses in Lark's barn got their vaccinations and the day off. She would be done by noon. And knowing Lark, she would be home, watching some show she couldn't watch when her daughter was around and inhaling junk food. Talk about bad timing.

"Fine." Ooo. I had an idea. "But it will be on your dime."

Dorothy's eyebrows crept up before she smiled. "High Tea?" We'd gone to the Tea House enough for her to guess. We had bonded years ago over our love of tea, and she was one of the few people in town that understood what it was like to deal with businesspeople at the level I did. Over the years, we had grown close.

I smiled. Well, it was more like a happy grimace, but it was the best I had at the moment. Maybe I could buy some shoes tonight, too. Tea and shoes. My comforts. Wait! No shoes. No more shoes until I had a source of income.

"I'll make the reservation." Dorothy winked at my capitulation.

Well, I wouldn't get much work done tomorrow, but at least I wouldn't be at home focused on Henry's death. Plus, I deserved a day to… Oh god. Dorothy had called it. I didn't know how to grieve. I knew how to throw myself into work. But my work would just remind me of my loss. Plus, what was I going to do? Tell people he was dead? All day?

Or maybe it was time I threw myself into something different? Or a giant brown-haired someone?

Okay. That was a bad thought. Bad, bad, dirty, trouble-creating thought. *No Nic, brain. No.*

"Grandmother." A handsome man, maybe a little over six foot, came over to us, a slight frown on his face; his stride showed that he was clearly agitated. He had expensive shoes, probably real leather, that matched the suit that fitted him like it was made for his body alone. This was a man who knew good shoes and good clothing. Too bad he was frowning.

"Kenneth. Donald. How nice to see you today," Dorothy greeted, with a fond smile.

Nice Shoes stopped to give Dorothy a kiss on her cheek and I saw the second man, following in Nice Shoes' shadow. Short, grumpy, and unremarkable. He did have the same brown hair and brown eyes of Nice Shoes, but without any of the pleasant features.

To be fair, they both were frowning. It was unfair to excuse one's unhappiness just because he was more attractive. Then again, my mentor had just died. I was allowing myself a little bit of unfair judging. Dumpy followed Nice Shoes' example, dropping a kiss on Dorothy's cheek, although I noticed Dumpy's lips hadn't actually touched her.

"Jen, these are my grandsons. Kenneth—" She pointed to Nice Shoes. "—And Donald." She pointed to Dumpy.

"Don. Please," Donald interrupted, thrusting his hand out in front of his brother's. Kenneth fell back with a sigh, letting his brother shake my hand first. I guessed that it wasn't the first time Donald had cut Kenneth off. What a charmer.

"Nice to meet you." Maybe. He looked me up and down before his smile grew broader. I guessed he liked what he saw. Gross. I turned to Kenneth, who also offered me his hand but without a word. Just a nod. He wasn't a talker.

"Grandmother. We have a problem," Kenneth said, turning away from me.

I'd been dismissed. Fun.

Her face sobered up, and she glanced at me. I could guess the problem.

"The police are handling it," she said, reaching out to wrap my shoulders in a comforting half hug. Kenneth's face softened slightly, as he realized I knew the victim.

"The guests are starting to notice. We need to get it contained. The police have cordoned off the entire floor. They have checkpoints. How do we control this?" he asked quietly. His words were insensitive, but his soft tone and sympathetic glances made me forgive him. The world kept moving. Business kept going. Just because my world was shaken didn't mean that they needed to stop theirs.

"My friend's business partner has been killed, basically in front of her. We will allow the police to do what they need to so they can solve this as soon as possible." She gave my shoulder another squeeze. "Plus, Lindsey will tell everyone in about five minutes, anyway."

"Who?" Kenneth asked, his eyes narrowed.

"Lindsey—" Her voice stopped when her phone alarm went off. "Hmm." She pulled it out and looked. "She's early. It's good to know she is on top of things."

"Town blog." I filled him in. "We couldn't support a paper, so Lindsey took it over in a blog form a few years ago. She's how all the town gets their news." And gossip. She added that in for free.

Kenneth looked like he wanted to say something, but glanced at me and closed his mouth, giving us both a sharp nod before spinning and walking away. Donald stayed behind, shifting his weight anxiously.

"Grandmother, do you have a minute?" Donald sent me a dismissive glance, trying to catch Dorothy's attention. "I wanted to talk to you again about my ideas for the—"

"Not now, Donald. Maybe later? I really need to be here for Jen right now."

And the gossip. I wasn't kidding myself on what my value to her was.

"But the special project isn't going to be available for long—"

"Not right now. Jen, honey, what are you doing tonight? Should the girls and I come over and help you mourn?"

Not going to happen.

"I'm sorry, Dorothy. I'm… busy…"

"Working with me on the case." Nic came around the corner.

Nic for the save. When did Satan switch to being on my side? Did I sell my soul to get it?

"Yes. Sorry, Dorothy. Got to help the police." Fingers crossed for good luck that they were leaving.

"Perfect. I'm just worried about you." Dorothy gave me the eye. The one that said she had a goal, and I was a part of it. "Donald was just commenting on how he wanted to see more of the town." Donald startled slightly at the mention before looking at me again, this time with more calculation in his eyes.

No. Really. No. "Not today. I need to…" What was my excuse again?

"Work with the police." This time Nic said it slower with a frown. Like he was leading me toward an answer.

Maybe trying to get the lie stuck in my head?

"Well, then, maybe when you are up to it?" She beamed at us both, but for some reason I felt like the smile was aimed more at Nic. Plus, shouldn't she be upset that I turned down her over-the-top matchmaking scheme? They never let Lark get away with saying no.

I tried not to take another look at Donald, mostly because I was afraid my complete lack of interest would show. Answer. I needed to answer.

"Fine. Another time." I sighed. I could always say no later.

Donald seemed indifferent, or maybe he didn't look disappointed because he took my answer as a yes? Either way, Nic seemed to guess I was just delaying and shook his head at my weakness. He had a point. I was being a pushover.

"Great! See you tomorrow, Jen." Dorothy swept away, Donald giving me a smile and a nod before following.

"Am I a horrible person for not wanting to go out with him?" I asked Nic.

"You mean, short and grumpy? Do you like short men?" he asked, looking truly curious.

"He isn't that short," I defended. I wasn't sure why. He kind of was.

Nic shook his head. "What are your plans for today?"

"I need to... wait. Why?" I looked at him through narrowed eyes. As of a few minutes ago, I had new plans. Ones that involved some wine. Maybe a cider or two.

"No reason," he said, eyes too wide, feigning innocence.

Well, my eyes weren't narrowed anymore, but that was only because my eyebrows were arched in suspicion.

"Am I expected to believe that?" I demanded.

"Well, there might be a few questions I want to ask you away from the hotel."

"Fine." No. My business partner just died. Murdered. Practically in front of me. "No, I'm not answering any more questions today. Tomorrow morning. But I need to be back here before eleven." I would help them. I would, just not today.

"You're going to make me a liar—"

"Jen!" A woman in a fashionable yellow sundress ran at me from the side, the matching hat falling behind her as she slammed into me. As I swayed, I noticed Nic sliding into the background. Close enough to hear, but not obviously a part of the group. Coward. "Can you believe that he's dead? They just told me. To think that we were down at brunch while it happened." Her arms enveloped me in a hug that I struggled to breathe through.

"Charlotte? What are you doing here?" Because I was pretty sure that Henry and his ex-wife were not vacationing partners. In fact, they had never vacationed together when they were married.

Also, we needed to talk about how short that sundress was, because I didn't know that anything needed to show off that much skin. It was late fall, so it wasn't like she was worried about being too hot. Her legs were fantastic, though. I was sure the surgeon that gave them to her was happy with the results.

Oops. That was mean, too. I wasn't a good person today.

"Henry told us that he got three suites at the resort for the weekend and invited all of us. As a family. I didn't know…" She looked away, bringing her hand to cover her mouth as if she was holding back a cry. For some reason, I had trouble believing it. Maybe it was the way it was artistically done, as if she had practiced it in the mirror. Maybe it was the way she had screamed how she hated him in the lobby of Henry's office before the divorce.

"He had three suites?" Wow. For a man who hated to vacation and never upgraded anything, three suites were a big expense. I mean, he told me that he wanted, just once in his life, to stay in a nice suite, but he always said he would do it after he retired. As his gift to himself. Then again, he had been looking at jail time, so maybe that was it.

"Yes. Frank and I are on another floor, though."

Funny, I didn't see any tears anymore. Guess she was over her despair.

"Where is Frank?" I asked, not able to think of anything less polite.

Charlotte's mouth went flat, and her eyes squinted in anger. "He was supposed to be at brunch with me and some friends, but he decided, last minute, that he had something better to do. He took his car and left for who knows where. We were just finishing up brunch when we heard the news. Our reservation got messed up and we had to go earlier than expected. This hotel is just not up to our standards."

"How horrible for you to be stood up like that." I tried to keep my face impassive, hiding my anger at her complaint against Dorothy's resort.

"He left before we even sat down and still hasn't come back yet. I've been calling him but he won't pick up. Children! You are so smart not to want to have any."

Ouch. I smiled politely at her dig at my unmarried, childless status. Frankly, I would rather pretend that I was single by choice than admit to this woman that I was failing in my personal life. Plus, I had a potential date with Grumpy sometime in the future. Maybe he was shy, and that's why his grandmother was setting him up.

Wine. Wine would make this all feel less overwhelming. Maybe a cocktail? This was quickly heading into cocktail category. And it was all waiting on the other side of town. I could do this. I could be polite to the somewhat grieving widow of my business partner.

"Yes. I'm sure." I nodded like I agreed, and she kept going.

"Did Henry tell you anything? I know he was supposed to talk to you today." She focused on me, trying hard to read my face.

"No. He was…" I stopped, taking a deep breath to control the tears and tried again. "No, I didn't get there in time."

That made her pause for a second before she hugged me, then pulled back. Thirty seconds of empathy. That was pretty good for her. After the hug, she pulled herself up, looking away as she went back into her distraught wife act.

"We were being investigated again. Can you believe that? Henry wanted to keep you in the dark. He said that this one was a false claim, and that you didn't need to worry about it, but I disagreed. You should know everything. Transparency. That's what they call it, right?"

"Yes." Henry was trying to keep me out of the investigation? I was... hurt? Relieved? Something like that. Another thing to process later. With my good friend Captain Morgan®. Yep, I was escalating, but it was starting to be a liquor kind of day.

Also, who was this 'we'? When did Charlotte and Henry start talking again?

"They accused another one of his clients of insider trading."

"No," I murmured soothingly.

"And what's worse..." Charlotte leaned in to whisper as if she was confiding a secret. "What's worse is that Henry had records of deposits from extra payments in one of the business accounts. Ones that the business couldn't account for."

"No." I didn't have to fake my surprise this time. That information stunned me. I had to fight my instinct to look at Nic. His choice to hide in the background was starting to make more sense. Wait, were we working as a team?

I pulled back a little as I processed. Henry was one of the top CPAs in the state. We both were exceptional at our jobs. That was why people paid us huge bucks. How did a CPA of Henry's caliber, if helping with illegal dealings, not cover his tracks for illegal payouts? Had Henry degraded that badly, and I hadn't noticed?

"Yes. Can you believe that? He was taking payments to look the other way."

Then why did he allow the account to get transferred to me? If he was taking payments? Something wasn't right.

"That's horrible," I answered, knowing better than to ask her any of the questions floating in my brain.

"You want to know what's even *worse?* That horrible Dan Ellson is in this hotel. This very weekend. I bet you he did it. He was screaming at Henry at the office in the city last week. Yelling that he believed Henry was the one who had turned him in. If anyone was going to kill Henry, it would be him." She brought her hand up, but this time it went to her chest. "He even accused Henry of turning him in last night in the lobby."

Too bad she didn't have pearls to clutch. I bet she was regretting that.

Also, why was Dan Ellson, a client of Henry's from San Francisco, here, in Barrow Bay? And what were the chances that they would all be here at the same time as Henry and his family?

"I'm sure the police will look into that," I murmured, still fighting not to look at Nic.

"And that nasty FBI agent is here. Let me know if he bothers you, dear. Do you have a good lawyer?" She patted my shoulder, opening her mouth to continue, but I cut in.

"Yes."

"I can give you—" She stopped mid-sentence when my answer processed. "You already have a lawyer?"

"Yes. I had some legal questions, and he's been helping me. Thank you for your offer, though." I was careful to keep my face even and polite. Right that moment, I wished I was more assertive. Blunt, even. My honest answers were sitting in my chest wanting to burst out and tell her how fake I found her.

But filters were a good thing. Professional. Lucrative. Polite. *Boring.*

"Well then, I guess we'll be seeing you around?" she muttered absently, probably still processing that I had a lawyer.

"You'll be staying at the hotel after what happened?" I asked, shocked.

"The police won't let us leave," she said, narrowing her eyes.

I could see that. If I didn't know that Charlotte would never lower herself to fire a gun, I would suspect her first. The police didn't know that Charlotte would never take the risk of gun powder staining. She would hire an assassin before doing it herself. Plus, she would've killed him before the settlement. She gained nothing in killing him now.

"I guess I'll be seeing you around." I smiled and started to wave before I stopped. "Charlotte?" I waited until I had her full attention again. "Do you know why Henry didn't tell me he was coming? Or why he would take a vacation in the middle of the investigation?"

Her body softened, and she looked at me with sad eyes. "He felt that he'd disappointed you. He wanted to tell you sorry in person. He was so proud of you, Jen. You were like a daughter to him. The thought that he had destroyed what the two of you had built... it hurt him more than the shame of being caught." With that, she turned and left.

I collapsed onto the couch again. He had been proud of me. I was a daughter to him. And I turned him in. My face dropped into my hands as the sob I was trying to hold back threatened to come up. The cushions next to me dipped and Nic's large hand started rubbing my back.

"Sometimes the people we love aren't who we want them to be."

"They never are," I mumbled. The tears leaked out, but the sob stayed stuck in my chest.

I wasn't sure how long we sat like that, but he didn't push it. Just let me breathe and fight down my despair.

Okay. That was enough self-pity. I had things to do. A plan.

I just had to remember what it was.

CHAPTER 6

I went home and got drunk. It wasn't a healthy reaction. Or particularly smart. But I was a happy drunk, and so for five hours I forgot about all my worries. I watched romantic comedies and drank. I texted Lark, who had a family dinner, and made plans for tomorrow. I ate a gourmet cake that I picked up from Dough & Nuts, our local bakery and nut shop. Turned out that white wine didn't go with chocolate cake very well, so I switched to champagne. Then it turned out that champagne was a good way to get a hangover. That's why the next morning, I was still sleeping when my doorbell rang.

I shot straight up in the air, my eyes snapping open, only to be covered with my hands when the sunlight made my headache worse.

Advil… Advil. I knew I put it around here somewhere. There. Popping two, no three, into my mouth and swallowing, I took the glass of water with me to answer the door.

"What?" I snapped, my hand covering my eyes. After a second of silence, I peeked. There was a man holding a to-go cup.

"Here." He shoved it at me.

Wolverine? No, Satan? Wait. I was calling him Cyclops now, wasn't I? Whatever. Nicknames could wait until I had less of a hangover.

"Nic?" I blinked up at him, hoping my eyes could handle the sunlight. I was wrong. "What is it?" I asked, looking down at the cup.

"I don't know. The tall, mouthy girl took one look at us, shoved it at me, and said you would need it."

Lark had brought me something? I calculated the odds it was coffee. No, I remembered some pretty drunk texts last night. On second thought, maybe coffee wasn't a bad idea. I brought it closer to smell. Vanilla and black tea hit my nose. It was my favorite tea from her grandmother's shop. Wow. She had to have gotten up early and made some pretty hefty promises to get this. I loved her.

"Thank you." I took a sip. "Now, why are you here?"

"You asked. We got it."

"Got what?" Oh. The warrant. In his hand. Well, my squinting wasn't working great, but I was pretty sure that it was the warrant in his hands. Fabulous.

"Drink too much last night?" he asked.

In my head there was a smirk, but I wasn't risking sunlight exposure to see.

"How could you tell?" I scowled, before turning and walking into the house, leaving the door ajar. That was as much of an invitation as I was able to give today. Was I wearing a bra this time? I looked down. Yes. Sports bra. Still needed to keep an eye on my thoughts, though.

"Was that a good idea?" Nic asked, following behind me into the kitchen.

"You mean, should I have gotten piss drunk the night before the FBI served a warrant to search my office and house? No. Not at all. But that's what I did." And I regretted it. So much. The champagne had been a bad call. And not enough water. Amateur mistakes. I knew hydration was key. One of the more practical things I had learned in college.

"Did you already take some Advil?" he asked, standing too close to me. I nodded, and he lifted my head so he could see my face. Probably because he didn't believe me, but my hormones jumped up and took control. My heart started to race, and my eyes settled on his mouth and refused to move. They were big. His lips, I mean. And his arms. I had felt his muscles when he held me yesterday. What big arms he had. I was suddenly wishing I had a little red hood to wear. I tore my eyes away from his lips to his eyes. The blue on the outside rim seemed deeper, locking me in as they searched mine. All I had to do was just reach up and I could—

"You like me."

Hit him. Hard. Maybe punch? Wait, Lark told me that hurt if you don't do it right. I couldn't afford to break my hand.

"You are too cocky for words," I replied, breaking away from his grasp and crossing my arms over my chest.

"You think I'm pretty," he smirked, his eyes tracking my escape.

"Pretty cocky." His smile widened. Why? Oh. "Don't say it."

"What? That I have something co—"

"No." I sent him the best glare I could come up with.

He lifted one eyebrow again.

No, not the eyebrow. Damn all those late nights watching classic *Star Trek* episodes. I watched too many old reruns.

"Why are you here bothering me?" I hissed. I was all kinds of sexy this morning.

"Warrant, remember?"

Why had I thought drinking last night was a good idea? *Henry. Dead. Insider trading. Life ending.* Okay. I remembered.

"Fine. What do you want me to get?"

"No need for you to help. My team is working on it right now." That was when I noticed all the other people in my house. That would teach me to keep my eyes closed when the FBI showed up. They had done that last time, too. Just appeared out of nowhere, without a sound. Or at least one that my stressed out, drunk senses registered.

On the other hand, drunk/hungover me was able to relax enough to really appreciate their snazzy FBI jackets. Okay, that was kind of cool. I didn't know how I missed appreciating how cool they were the first time they searched. Maybe I could join the FBI? Maybe being a snitch would be a good thing in their eyes. And I would get a jacket. I needed a change in career. Did guys find female FBI agents as sexy as we found the men?

"Do I need to be here?" From my understanding, they could have access to anything in the house, since I had my office in my spare bedroom. I couldn't stop them, but I didn't need to make Nic's life easier. Let them waste their time trying to find something that wasn't there. My files were clean. I paid big bucks to my lawyer to make sure I was protected. Last time I was willing to stay and fight. Now? That part of me might have died with Henry.

"I have some more questions for you," Nic said, pulling out a chair and sitting down without waiting for my invite.

Did he just order me around? My head hurt too much for this.

Without speaking, I turned and headed to my room. I was still a little fuzzy from the hangover and I really wanted to be clean more than I wanted to answer questions.

"Where are you going?" he called out.

"I'm taking a shower."

"With fifteen people in your house serving a warrant?"

Oh, yeah. Maybe not. I wasn't as sober as I would want to be.

I stopped in the hallway, taking in the people in my home. They all smiled in greeting and were respectful of my stuff as they searched. It still felt wrong. Respectful searching. It just felt... surreal.

Nic drew my attention again, waving his notebook with what I assumed were his case notes. Helping the police solve the murder. I could do that.

Turning around, I took another sip of tea, letting the heat and caffeine rush through my system. I refused to acknowledge that I was wandering around in my pajamas, with my hair in who knew what condition, but my hand drifted up before I stopped it.

No wonder he ruined the moment with his stupid comment. I must have looked horrible.

Well, the damage was done. No sense in crying over it. I definitely didn't need to be any less hydrated.

"Okay. I'm ready. What do you want to know?"

"Did you know that Henry signed a document saying he, and he alone, helped Tony Harris cover up his illegal trades?"

Huh.

I froze. "Did he add the alone part?"

"Yes."

Henry was protecting someone. My brain tried to convince me it was me, but logic didn't follow. I hadn't done anything wrong and Henry knew it. Frank, however... Well, his record of making mistakes was longer than we would normally allow. I refused to let him work on any of my accounts after the fourth time he didn't do what I asked and I got an angry phone call. I had enough problems on my own. I wasn't covering for Frank.

Would Henry have... no. Not with an important account like Tony's. Henry wouldn't have let Frank work on Tony's account. Not when Harris corporation was one of our biggest customers. But I was starting to think he did. The weight in my chest got heavier.

I sat. It would be more accurate to say my knees gave out, because my conscious mind wouldn't just sit on the kitchen floor. I did manage to pull it off, though, by leaning against the wall. Like I meant to do it. What could I say? I was a boss.

"What do I have to do to know what is going through your brain?" Nic's voice interrupted my thoughts.

Looking up I found him on one knee, his other leg bent as he watched me process. One hand rested on his knee, but the other hovered by my arm as if he wanted to touch, but didn't know if I'd allow it. I wouldn't. Okay, maybe I'd had one or two dreams last night of his hands on me, but not right now.

On the other hand, he just asked me what he had to do. My evil side decided to cover for my other sides, who were reeling from Nic's words.

"Hop three times on one foot, spin around and rub your belly five times."

He just looked at me for a few minutes. Yep. I surprised him with that one. Then he started to get up. Uh oh. Needed to up the stakes.

"Naked." *What?* Talk about a Freudian slip.

His chin dropped. Well, well. Didn't expect that, did he? Ha. I won.

Then he slowly smiled at me. No, smiled wasn't right. Smirked was not enough, either. Was there a smugger option? I couldn't think of one. I watched in fascinated horror as his hands went to his belt. No. He wouldn't. I looked up at his face, my mouth hanging. I had an open floor plan, so the kitchen was pretty open to the rest of the house. Surely, there was no way he would go that far into unprofessionalism with his coworkers watching?

"It's for the case. Us *information whores* do what it takes."

Huh. That comment really got to him. But there at least were fifteen of his colleagues in my house. He wasn't going to strip.

I was pretty sure.

I offered him my best bravado smile. It might have been a little shaky. I was emotionally exhausted. And still very hungover.

"Do you think your friends will let me record it? For promotional reasons?" I asked. *Damn*. I had balls when hungover. Or I was still drunk. I thought about it for a second. I just gave a sexual advance to an FBI agent who was investigating me. Yep, I was leaning toward still drunk. Hungover me generally still listened to the filter that was screaming in my head that this was beyond the bounds of professionalism.

"You think the FBI would want it? You think I'm that hot?" Nic's smirk got wider.

"No. I was talking about for me. To show customers what lengths I go to protect their information." Ha. Another frown, this time almost making me think I might have hurt his feelings. Nah, I was pretty sure he didn't have any feelings.

On another note, this may be why I was still single.

He recovered quickly. "You sure it wouldn't be for your own *purposes*?"

Gasp.

He did not… no.

"I never." I jumped to my feet, arms flailing in his direction. "You take that back!"

"You never, huh?" He looked me up and down. "That explains a lot."

Done. I was done.

"Out. Get. Out!"

"I have a warrant."

Good point. "Then I'll leave."

"Fine."

"Fine."

I grabbed my car keys and walked to the garage door, dodging FBI agents who had stopped to stare at us. I didn't blame them. If it hadn't been me, I would've been staring, too.

Unlocking my car by remote, I grabbed the door and swung it open with all my might. Which made no noise. *Unsatisfying.* I slammed it closed.

Bang.

There. That was what I wanted. He knew I was mad. The whole house knew I was mad.

And in my pajamas.

Hmm, I might have not thought this through. Was I even sober enough to drive? That conversation in there would indicate not.

Well, I wasn't going back in now. I stuck my key in the ignition and lifted my hand to open the garage door before hesitating. Maybe I could borrow some clothes? Or maybe buy some new ones? Yeah. Not so much. I didn't even have shoes on.

I couldn't leave.

Not without shoes.

Or admitting that some of that was my fault. I was a grown woman. I couldn't blame the alcohol or the hangover. As much as I wanted to. My filter had told me that was a bad move and I had chosen to ignore it in favor of getting one over on Nic.

Stupid.

Plus, I did want to help with solving Henry's murder.

I was stuck between my ego and my pride. I would've thought that I was a bigger person than that by this age. I sighed and let my head drop to rest on the steering wheel. I had no idea what to do.

I glanced down at my phone when the text alert went off. Lindsey had posted another blog. My fingers shook as I stared at the phone, debating opening it. It had to be about Henry. Or me. Or both of us. Or the insider trading. Or the FBI. Look at me, giving her so many options for her blog. Maybe she could cut me in on her profit.

Okay. I was going to look. I worked better when I had all the information.

Cake Configuration Causes Chaos.

Huh. Well, that was definitely not about me. Should I look? I mean, I was having a moment right here with my own stupidity. Should I stop it to read about someone else's? *Yes.*

> *Today at eight am, two men in a state of questionable sobriety entered Dough & Nuts, reportedly trying to buy a cake in the shape of a female sex organ. When the shop owner refused, the discussion became heated about what types of cakes the shop would provide for an extra fee. Rumor is that expletives and threats were involved, causing one of the co-owners to step in, physically throwing the men out of the store, where they landed on a passerby. The only witness to the altercation and the unfortunate recipient of the two men, then fled the scene. The witness remains elusive, even though we did try to get her statement before she managed to slip away to the resort. She was in impressive physical conditioning as she ran the entire distance, some three miles, from the shop to the resort, but don't worry, readers. I will keep trying to find her and get more details.*

Egad. Lindsey tried to get her statement, but the witness escaped with impressive physical conditioning? That could only mean one thing. The poor girl from the resort witnessed an argument about a cake in the shape of a female body part and then was run down by our local blogger with too much commitment and not enough supervision.

I could picture it. The poor thing getting stuck in the middle of the cake craziness, being hit by flying men, only to be followed by a big-boobed girl with very little running experience. I watched Lindsey attempt the last Barrow Bay marathon. It wasn't pretty. I mean, she knew how to walk. That should have given Lindsey some instinct for running, right? It didn't. Somewhere on the resort was a traumatized girl who was going to have nightmares of cakes in the shape of body parts and flying limbs.

I couldn't help it. I laughed, the soul-deep laugh releasing the stress and emotions I was suppressing. I loved this town.

Less panicked now that someone else was having a worse day than me, I noticed the door leading into the house was still open, and I could see Nic getting chewed out by a tiny woman in an FBI jacket. Like, small. Maybe five foot? Or it could just be that she was standing next to Nic. She was waving her arms around and Nic was standing there, his arms crossed and a frown on his face. I craned my head a little more to get a better look. Yep. She was really yelling. And he wasn't saying a word. After a second, she pointed behind him and he turned and left.

I guess she won.

She turned and approached my car, stopping on the passenger side to knock on my window. From this angle, I could tell that she was older than me, maybe in her forties, and had pretty brown eyes that sparkled with amusement. Good. I was glad someone was getting a laugh out of this.

"Hi," I offered once I rolled the window down.

"Hi." She glanced around at my car. "You seem to get under Nic's skin."

Okay.

She waited for a response, but I was stuck in my anger. Too stuck to say anything. Or maybe it was embarrassment. I was having an epically bad week. I didn't need to look at it too closely. Sometimes mental stability was really just not looking too hard at the details of life. After she waited a few seconds, she kept going.

"Where are you going?"

"Somewhere."

"In pajamas?"

"Looks like it." I wasn't backing down. Well, I was pretending I wasn't backing down.

"You sure you don't want to change? And get some shoes?"

Yes! But no one did favors for free. "What's it going to cost me?"

"You are very suspicious for someone so young," she commented.

"Twenty-nine isn't that young," I said bitterly.

"Ahh. You starting to feel old?" she asked with a nod. "I remember when I turned thirty. No children. No husband. No boyfriend in sight." She sighed. "It sucks being married to the job."

"Yep." I sank lower in my seat before I looked at her. "What did you do?"

"Nothing. Still no children. No husband. I have a boyfriend now, but he's always busy."

"I was kind of hoping for you to say something uplifting. Like you were married and happy and that being old isn't the end of the world."

She winced. "Sorry. Does it help that I like my life? Even without what I was told I should want, I'm happy."

Not really.

I looked back out my front window at my garage wall. There was nothing on it. I never had the time to do anything out here. Who was I kidding? I wouldn't have decorated the house if Lark hadn't made me. And brought Janet, her interior decorator cousin, with her.

"You ever thought of quitting?" I asked, hoping the question wasn't too revealing. Then again, I had no food in my kitchen. Still. I was guessing they knew I was pathetic.

"A few times. But when you love something, giving up isn't always the answer. Sometimes, finding a new way to enjoy what you love gives you back more."

"Wow. You sold yourself short on the whole uplifting quote section of this talk."

She laughed, shaking her head. "I stole it from a book. But it's true. I switched departments. I travel less. Work on what I enjoy, not just what makes me surface happy." She shrugged. "I annoy cocky coworkers that think too highly of themselves."

I winced, since I was pretty sure who she was talking about.

"I'm sorry about being so unprofessional in there."

"Please. We pulled up at your door at nine a.m. the morning after you lost your business partner. Hungover was the best of the potential options we could have had. Plus, we recorded your argument. The information whore bit was priceless." She smiled, and I heard a chuckle from inside the house somewhere.

I was never going to be able to look at any of the agents in the eye again. Good thing they were all going home.

Glancing over, I saw that she was still leaning against the car, waiting for me to make a decision.

"I can really come in and get dressed?" I asked, tentatively feeling my head for how bad the situation was. Bad. My hair was bad.

"I will even kick the guys out if you want to take a shower."

"I love you," I breathed.

"I know." She winked as she turned to leave.

"Wait. Was that a Star Wars reference?" I yelled out, but she was gone.

Okay. *Time to face the music.* I got back out of my car, slipping my purse on my arm. I didn't remember grabbing the purse while storming out, so I was impressed by my muscle memory. Walking slowly toward the door, I was unsettled by the fact that my feet made no noise as I walked. No heels. I always wore heels out here. I hesitated for a second at the door, then pushed myself to step in.

I was a brave, strong, capable, independent woman. I could take a shower and get dressed in the same house with the investigative team. And I could do it with my head held high. So high that I couldn't meet anyone's eyes. Yes. That was the plan. Fake pride and don't meet anyone's eyes.

With no heels.

CHAPTER 7

Showered and dressed, I left my room to find a subdued Nic waiting for me in the hall. I should apologize. I escalated that situation past professional bounds. He already got yelled at. I should—

"You ready to answer some questions now?"

—not say a thing. Because he was the enemy. The people who were trying to shut my business down. He was ruining my life. Destroying my sanity. Solving my partner's murder?

Okay, that went too far. It wasn't even logical. They weren't trying to shut down my business, just find criminals. That happened to be customers. And my partner.

I really needed to stop overreacting because I was angry that Henry did this. Or guilty that I turned him in.

"Whatever," I answered with a glare. A small one. Because he did just get chewed out. And I was trying to stop overreacting. Small steps.

"Will you tell me what you were thinking about?"

93

"Nope," I answered. I said it a little to be contrary, but mostly because I wasn't sure, and I didn't know what to do with the information.

"Please?"

"I believe my best option at this point is to stay silent. If you have any questions, you should ask my lawy—"

"Don't say it."

Huh. Maybe I did have some power here. All I had to do was ask for my lawyer. "What do I get if I don't?"

"That's not how this works." He frowned, crossing his arms for emphasis.

"Okay, then. You should address all your questions to my—"

"Okay, what do you want?" he asked, his hand dragging through his hair and messing it up. He looked better a little messed up.

"A question for a question."

"No. That's not how this works." He shook his head like that was the final say.

"We already did that bit," I reminded him. Was he going to make me say it?

"Fine. What do you want to know?"

"Henry died. How?" I didn't really want to know, but the detail monster inside couldn't rest until I did. I needed to know the specifics. Where he was shot. How. Why. All the information. Information was the key to solving any question.

"Gunshot wound, close quarters, to the chest." He waited for my nod before continuing. "How long did it take you to figure out Tony's trading?"

"Two months. The first month I was suspicious. I started looking into past trades in my spare time. By the second month, I had another trade and a pattern. I reported it and advised Henry that I was dropping his account due to conflicts with my work for their business account."

"Did he protest?"

"No. No, he didn't." Why hadn't that seemed weird at the time? I was just too relieved to question it when it happened. Now I realized I should have questioned it. I had been so dumb.

"And did you know anything about Dan?"

"No. I never saw any of his records. I knew he was a client, but that's it." I watched as he wrote that down.

"Why didn't you start breaking away from the business?" he asked softly.

"Because I didn't want it to be real," I whispered. "Henry... he was like a father to me. I didn't want to believe..." I stopped talking and sank to the floor. On the ground. Again. Twice in one day. This was probably symbolic of my life.

"I'm sorry." Nic sat beside me, studying the pictures on my walls. They were all contemporary. Lark liked to complain about how awful they were, but I loved them. How the designs used beauty to evoke passion, make points, change minds. It was amazing.

Nic looked like he didn't agree with me.

"It was a good question. I should have. I was stupid," I admitted.

We sat in silence for a few seconds.

"Was anything taken from the room?" I asked, remembering how his stuff was spread out.

"Not that we know of." He hesitated. "Did you know he was sick?"

"No. How did you know?"

"He had medication in his room. And at his home."

"I had no idea. What did he have?" Turned out Henry was keeping a lot of things from me. So much for trust.

"We don't know yet. We were hoping you would."

"I had no idea. I had no idea about a lot of things." I didn't hide the bitter note there.

Maybe it was me. The reason all the men in my life turned out to be liars. Maybe I chose to be around them. My dad. My ex. My partner. The common thread was me.

"Would it surprise you to know he was in contact with his ex-wife?"

"Before I saw her at the resort? It would've shocked me. No, it still does," I corrected myself. "They hated each other. She married for money and security. He married because she was hot. Then it was too expensive to divorce. Until she slept with a client. Then she was a liability." Maybe Henry wasn't that great of a judge of character, either.

"So, the divorce was bitter."

"Very."

We sat there for a moment, both lost in thought, pretending to look at my paintings.

"Does the name Scarlett Johansson mean anything to you?"

"Like the actress?" I glanced over at him really quick, but I couldn't tell anything from his face.

"Yes."

"No. Definitely not a client. Loved her stuff though. Why?"

"He was in contact with someone by that name in the past few weeks, but we don't see any reference to, well, anything." His head shook slightly, as if it was an unconscious reveal of his frustration.

"What?" That didn't make any sense. Henry wasn't much of a small talk guy unless you paid him to be.

"It's a string of emails about how nice their days were. Nothing else."

"Their days," I repeated.

"Yes. Weather conditions. Temperatures. That kind of stuff."

"I've no idea. I'm guessing it wasn't the real Scarlett Johansson?"

"No."

Silence.

"You know, me saying that you should talk to my lawyer wouldn't have stopped you talking to me. Just your questions," I pointed out, letting my head fall back to rest on the wall. Mostly because it just occurred to me. "It would be up to me to stay quiet." And pay the lawyer bill.

"I know. But you felt more in control when you thought it would, didn't you?"

"Devious." Sexy. No, I did not just think that. *Bad brain.* "Would you really have let me leave?"

"No. We had cars blocking you in, too." He shot me a gloating grin before looking forward again.

Well played.

"I have to be at the hotel by eleven to meet with Julia and her son."

He nodded. "You mind if I go with you?"

"Yes." I frowned. "Why?"

I got a shrug as he glanced away. It didn't tell me much, so I kept staring.

"I want to see more of the town."

More staring.

"Fine. Someone killed your business partner and we have no leads. John thought I might follow you around today and see if something stands out."

"That sounds like a long shot." And a little familiar.

He shrugged.

"You have no leads?" That didn't sound right.

Another shrug.

"What about Dan Ellson?" Nothing. Who else was there? "Charlotte has a few dozen people that can alibi her, so she is out."

"A hundred."

"What?"

"Charlotte had a hundred people that could alibi her at the time of the murder. She didn't leave the brunch until a few minutes after the murder."

"I thought she was told that he was dead at the brunch?"

His forehead wrinkled as he thought. "No. She was in the lobby, having just left the brunch. Still in sight of everyone though. All one hundred."

"That seems like overkill."

He was back to shrugging. "I guess that's the normal turnout for brunch, even during the week."

"Even during the off-season?"

"Yep."

"This town is so weird." I sighed. Their brunch must be amazing.

"I'm getting that impression."

"So Charlotte is out. Frank?" I asked.

"You think Frank might have done it? Why?" He eyed me, trying to figure out why I asked.

Why *did* I ask? I hadn't shared my thoughts that Frank might have been behind the cover up. I certainly didn't want to now.

"No reason. Just going through all the people." I gave him an extra shruggy shrug, playing it off.

"He left before the murder, but he said he just went for a drive."

"So, no real alibi."

"No," he sighed. "But there's no record of his car coming back until after the murder."

I pursed my lips in thought. He was right, they had no leads. It had to be Dan, or I was out of suspects. Or Frank, I guess. There had to be ways around the cameras.

"It has to be Dan."

"You would think." He agreed, but there was something unspoken.

"But?"

"But, you're a civilian. And you need to get to the resort to escort some lady and her kid around town." He looked over, doing his eyebrow thing. The one-up thing. I managed to stop my sigh. Barely. "Why are you escorting them, again?" he asked.

"Long story." Crazy story that wasn't going to make me look good, so I was definitely skipping sharing it. "Are you really going to follow me around all day?"

"No. I have some questions for the hotel manager. Just thought I would catch a ride with you."

"John suggested it, didn't he?"

"Yes. I said no."

I nodded. "You didn't bring your own car?"

"Rode over with a coworker."

Right. Why didn't I believe him? But I was too tired to argue, and it was almost eleven. Time to go.

"This is nice," he commented, and I looked at him, my brow furrowed.

"What's nice?" *If he says the murder discussion, I might have to hit him and take my chances in court.*

"Us. Not fighting." He snuck a peek at me, but I was too surprised at his answer to know what he thought of my expression.

"It is," I admitted quietly, before jumping to my feet. That was enough for now. I needed to get away from him before I admitted something I couldn't take back. Like my dream last night.

I headed to the car, while he moved the cars parked behind me out of the way. They really had blocked me in. Was there something wrong with me that the planning to block me in before they knocked impressed me?

Probably.

Finally, all the cars were gone and Nic had joined me. As we pulled out, I was lost in my own thoughts, a round robin of processing Henry's death, trying to understand why someone would do it, and trying to figure out how to lure Julia into staying. Nic seemed to be okay with it since he didn't say anything, either. The drive was quick and I found a parking spot near the front, which I hoped wasn't an indication that they had people leave after yesterday's murder. Though I had to admit, I would feel weird vacationing in the same building that someone died in the day before.

"Are you going to follow me in?" I asked Nic.

"Just to the hotel. Then I need to meet with Kenneth. He's running point for the resort and our teams with regard to the murder."

Interesting. I guessed that was a clear indication who was going to be running the hotel in the future.

I got out of the car and Nic quickly followed. I had about ten minutes until I was supposed to meet Julia and Logan, so I headed to the lobby as Nic wandered over to the front desk. Sitting on the same couch as yesterday, I tried to come up with an official letter to send to our clients telling them what happened. I had gotten two sentences in when a voice interrupted me.

"Jen. I'm so glad I ran into you."

I looked up to see Frank standing there, smiling the same smile I used to see on Henry's face. They looked a lot alike, Henry and his son. Same receding hairline. Same brown eyes. Same wide smile. Same husky frame, although it looked better on the older man than on the one who was still in his twenties, even if only by one year. But where Henry's eyes had been wide and welcoming, Frank's were beady and mean. Okay, that might've been me projecting, but it was all I could see. The cruel streak that I knew was there even though he had never shown it to me. I stood, not comfortable with him hovering above me.

"Hello, Frank. I'm so sorry for your loss." His smile wavered slightly when he remembered he was supposed to be mourning. But it didn't leave completely.

"It's been hard, but Mother and I are working through it. Thank you for your condolences. We have confidence that Dan will be arrested for the murder soon." He was still smiling, even if it was just slightly.

It was creepy.

They should definitely not have Frank speak at the funeral. At least Charlotte faked a few tears. How a sweet man like Henry had these people in his life, I would never understand.

Oh, wait. He might have been helping a criminal and hiding things from me. Maybe it wasn't that hard to believe.

No. No, it was. It was hard to reconcile the man I knew with the Henry who was being painted in the last few days. Which was the truth?

"Henry's loss will be felt for a while." I didn't bother to remind him I was hurting, too. I was all about realistic expectations. "Did you want something?" I tried to keep my tone light and not let any of the bitterness escape. He didn't seem to notice.

"I wanted to talk to you about the business."

Oh. I should have predicted he would want to talk about that. I wasn't ready. Couldn't he see I wasn't ready? I looked away, forcing my eyes wide to dry any hidden tears.

"I've already started crafting a letter to our customers and contacted some firms to see who would have room for our clients." This time there was a definite clip to my tone, but he still ignored it.

"What if we didn't? I have a few resumes from CPAs that would be a good fit for the firm. We could hire someone and have them take over Dad's accounts. Until then, I can work under your supervision. I know I'm not a CPA, but I can do a lot of the accounting and I know all Dad's accounts inside and out. I can take on more responsibility. With you at the lead, we don't have to let Dad's dream die." His smile widened, and he stepped closer to me.

I stepped back.

"No. With the scandal from the second case of insider trading, the firm is done. I'm resigning and closing it down. Like I said, I've already started looking for potential matches for our clients. I'm sorry, but I just don't believe anyone will have faith in the name anymore."

"What if I told you I could guarantee some of our clients would stay with us? If we helped them with their special projects." His smile, the one that was so offensive already, turned even worse. Or maybe it was the way his eyes hooded. Either way, I suddenly was wishing Nic had come with me.

"Special projects?" I didn't like the sound of that. My suspicious mind, the one that was already thinking that Henry was covering up for Frank, was jumping to all kinds of conclusions. All of them revolved around Frank being the mastermind behind the insider trading. Which was ridiculous. Frank couldn't mastermind a dinner, much less a plot involving multiple people and hidden payments. It could be innocent. Maybe they just had a demanding project no one wanted to do. Which meant neither did I. "I don't think—"

"Don't answer me, now. Think about it."

I didn't need to. The answer was no. But I didn't want to have the confrontation now. I was too close to tears, too emotional from losing my friend, too anxious from the fear of losing my stability. I didn't have it in me to try and argue with him. Let him think there was a chance.

I let out a long breath when he left, scurrying away into the crowd. My gaze stayed on him as he stopped to talk with Donald Watts, which made me frown.

"You aren't going to do it, are you?" Kenneth Watts was suddenly beside me, watching Frank and Donald talk.

"You think it's a bad idea?" Not that I thought it was a good one.

"You seem like a competent person. One that should see through that." He pointed his head at Frank.

"I am." That was arrogant. "There is no chance the company will stay open."

He assessed me, his eyes thoughtful. "Interesting."

I had nothing to say to that.

Falling silent, we both looked across the lobby at the two men talking. Really, my company closing wasn't as interesting as those two knowing each other.

How would a worm like Frank know Donald, presumably an up-and-coming player in the extensive Watts empire? I guessed they both lived in San Francisco, so maybe they had run into each other, but that seemed very unlikely. The conversation didn't take long, and then Frank was gone, lost into the crowd of people getting onto the elevator.

My gaze returned to Donald as he watched Frank disappear. The grumpy grandson of yesterday was gone, but the person in front of me was even worse.

"Do you know how they know each other?"

Kenneth frowned. "No. But it can't be good." After that, he turned and walked away without saying goodbye. Once he was lost to a back room, my eyes returned to Donald.

Was I imagining things? Or was Donald Watts, grandson of Dorothy Watts and presumable heir to some of their business empire, a part of this? And how?

CHAPTER 8

It wasn't long after Frank left that I spotted Julia coming toward me, her blonde hair standing out in the crowd.

"Jen!" Surprised, I took a step as Logan hugged me. Apparently, he'd managed to sneak ahead of this mother. The hug, though... I couldn't grasp the emotions going through my mind as his little arms wrapped around my legs. Instead, I bent down to throw my arms around him.

I wanted this. I wanted children.

And for the first time in my life, I wanted it more than security. More than money. More than my job.

I was ready for love.

As I let myself glory in his trust, my mind started making plans.

New plans. Better plans.

I was done being anxious all the time. I was done with not having time to do anything but eat and sleep. There was more to life and I was going to get it.

This could be the grief talking, but life was short. Security didn't mean anything if I was dead.

Plans. I was secure. Well, I was secure enough. *If* I could control my anxiety and live without my expensive shoes. But if this was the reward, I could do it. I only needed fifty thousand a year to support my lifestyle. I could probably do that with a few small clients. Or maybe I would just do taxes for the locals. Who knew? But I was getting this.

My new plan:

Step One: get a date. I needed to go check my online profile since I hadn't looked at it in a month.

Step Two: get married. Hmm. That one might be optional, but preferable. I was a talented, amazing woman. I could raise kids on my own. That negated Step One, too.

Step Three: Have children. Two, maybe three. I would decide once I had one.

I broke away and looked at his smiling face. Yep. That was the plan. I had a goal and a plan. Nothing was going to stand in my way.

"You still going for that tour?" The deep voice startled me again. This was turning into a habit.

Satan had returned. Lucky me. And unfortunate timing, since my plan now had his face all over it. No. Nic was not a stay-in-one-place kind of person. He was a flirt. He was like my ex.

He could be another liar.

"Logan, have you met Nic? Nic was just *leaving*." I snapped out the last word, but Nic looked unconcerned. I needed to up my hissing game.

"Not anymore. My plans fell through so I thought I'd come and share in your tour. I would *love* to see the sights of exotic Burrow Bay."

"*Barrow* Bay," I hissed.

He shrugged.

I wished I had something to throw at him instead of just angry glances.

Julia, who had come up beside me during the interaction, looked amused. *Great.*

"This is your first time in town?" Julia asked Nic, who answered while still smiling at me.

"No. I travel a lot for work, and this is my second time here," Nic replied.

Yeah, I imagined sleepy little Barrow Bay wasn't on the FBI's hot list of crime cities. Though for three days, we did think we had *two* drug dealers. Turned out to be just one that managed to double his business, but we hadn't known that. And since he was murdered, I wasn't sure if we still had any. Sleepy might've been an overstatement of how calm our town really was.

"Well, you are welcome to come with us." Julia smiled warmly at him. "My family and I are thinking about moving here."

"Really? Where do you live now?"

"San Francisco."

"I was just there a few weeks ago."

"For a case?"

"How did you—" He cut himself off, giving her a suspicious look.

"Please. That suit *screams* FBI." She smiled at him, but it had a definite sly edge.

They both turned and looked at me. Oops. My snickering might have been a little too loud.

"What? You do look like an FBI agent," I defended my amusement.

"And what, pray tell, does an FBI agent look like?"

Uh oh. I looked at Julia for help.

"Handsome?" she offered, trying to placate him.

Not what I wanted, but probably a smarter option. "Shall we go get in the car?" I asked, deciding we should leave before I got myself into more trouble.

"Yes. Good idea." Julia turned toward the exit, snagging Logan, who had wandered off during our conversation. "I can't wait to see everything."

"You realize that there are only two blocks of everything, right?" I asked as I followed, leaving Nic to pull up the rear. Wait. I glanced behind me. Yep. He was staring at my rear. I sent him a warning glare that he ignored before I turned around to hide my blush along with the smile I was currently trying to deny. I was not going to find his... his... cocky, overconfident... *cockiness* sexy. He was a player, and I was too smart to fall for someone like him.

I also ignored Julia's amused glances. It was not what she thought. At all.

"Julia? You want to take the passenger seat so you can see better?" I asked, shooting Nic a warning. This was about Julia, not Nic.

"Oh, I couldn't. Nic is so much taller," Julia protested, wrapping her arm around her son.

"No, no. I insist," Nic said, returning my glare with a confident smile. Here was a man who didn't worry about anything. He knew he was sexy and was comfortable in his skin. He would never understand what it was like to stay up all night going over the same conversation over and over until *he* cried. In fact, I would bet he had never cried. Ever. He was probably one of those manly men who only grunted in pain. Tears probably refused to even come near his eyes.

"Jen! Nic! Julia!" Dorothy came flying out of the hotel walking at a pace faster than a person of her age should. But no one would dare say that to Dorothy Watts, widow of Gerald Watts, business magnate. Mother of two sons who continued to conquer the business world. Grandmother of… okay, I didn't know how many grandchildren she had, but there were at least two. "I'm so glad to see you all together."

Why… oh, seriously? She was checking up on us. Like I would let her down.

"I'm so glad you suggested this, Dee," Julia gushed.

"I'm glad, dear. I hope you have fun. Oh, and Jen?"

Oh, no. "Yes, Dorothy?"

"Do you have any plans for this evening? I just couldn't sleep last night thinking about you all alone, grieving your business partner. I know how close the two of you were."

I looked away, trying to swallow the lump in my throat. She was right. Over the years I had told her a lot of my life story, and Henry was a big part of it. "I'm doing okay. Really."

"Well, we can't let you be alone tonight." She glanced quickly at Nic for a second, as if she were hoping he might say something before continuing. "Donald was interested in taking you out. I will tell him to meet you at The Pub around six." Another glance at Nic, who was red in the face, but silent.

It didn't sound like a question. "No, Dorothy, I couldn't—"

"Nonsense. I know you. If left to your own devices, you would be at home drinking or working. No. A night out on the town is just what you need. I'll tell him you'll be there."

I held her stare for a second, believing I was going to do it, that I would say no, then caved. Damn it. She was right. I didn't want to be home alone tonight. And Lark was going to be busy with Hailey. Plus... what if Donald was *the one*? I had been choosing to skip so many options, could I really look myself in the eye if I said no? Dorothy knew me, she knew what I needed in a man. Maybe she really thought this might work?

I wasn't getting out of this. Lark got Captain America, and I got Grumpy.

I thought I was a good person. I reported crimes. I helped little old ladies. Where had I gone wrong?

I suddenly felt the need for alcohol. Why didn't I hit the bar before I came? Lots and lots of yummy day-forgetting alcohol. Or shoes. Louboutin store, here I come.

No. I need to save money. No shoes.

"Fine. I guess I could meet him for a drink." Maybe ask him a few questions about Frank. And how he knew him. Suddenly, I was more interested in that option. This line of questioning always worked for Lark.

Dorothy smiled, sending Nic another look, which he ignored. "I'm so excited. I just know *you all* will love Barrow Bay as much as we do." With that, she spun around and sailed back into the hotel before I could say anything.

Hold up. "You all?" There wasn't supposed to be a *you all*. Just a Julia and Logan. I narrowed my eyes at Nic, who was scowling after Dorothy.

"You all?" I repeated, doing my best version of his one raised brow. It wasn't as good as his, but he still frowned before shifting uncomfortably.

"Is Nic thinking about staying, too?" Julia asked, her smile telling me that she was enjoying this.

"I don't know. Let's ask him," I said with a fake smile and a tone that clearly told him we weren't moving until he fessed up.

He tried to out-glare me. It was cute. I've stared down CEOs and COOs since I got out of college. He was going down.

It took two minutes. Amateur.

"My boss asked that I accompany you. Specifically. On the tour. Specifically," he admitted.

"Specifically?"

"Specifically," he confirmed.

"Does your boss not like you?" I asked, eyeing him.

"No. She loves me."

"Are you bad at your job?"

"No, I'm the best." He looked very offended now. Too offended.

"Really?"

"Okay. Maybe more like top five."

"Burning out," Julia interrupted. "He's burning out."

"I'm not." Nic was now scarlet, but I couldn't tell if it was anger, embarrassment, or both. "I'm not burning out. I'm..." He trailed off, looking into the distance.

"You sure?" I asked, smiling smugly at him after he had been silent for too long. I had warned him.

"Yes."

"Then why did your boss just set you up?" I lifted both eyebrows in challenge. It was worth making sure he got the message.

His jaw worked as he tried to come up with an answer. I felt bad. No one wanted to face the realization that they weren't happy at their job. Or that their boss was thinking they needed to move on to another career. Or another life.

"Why do you think she's setting me up?" he finally asked.

"Dorothy needs a new chief of security at the hotel. Obviously, you are who they came up with. It makes sense. They like to pick their people, and they already knew you."

His jaw was still working, although it included more gaping this time. I guess no one had told him the truth yet. Oops. Guess their plan might have just gotten shot down and he would have to go home where he wouldn't mess with my dreams anymore. Oh well.

Suddenly he turned and walked away, reaching for the passenger side door and ripping it open before he slumped into the car and slammed it shut.

"Guess I get the back," Julia commented.

"That was a lot of truth," I sighed.

"You *were* a little blunt."

"He's here investigating me and my late business partner for fraud." I wasn't feeling bad. I wasn't.

"Did you do it?"

"No."

"Did your partner?"

"Maybe," I conceded.

"You like Nic." Julia wiggled her eyebrows at me.

"Maybe." Wait. "No. I meant no." Sneaky rapid-fire questions.

She just smiled and got Logan in the car before getting settled herself.

Well, that didn't go the way I wanted it to.

"Hey, Jen!"

Jumping at any excuse to not get into the car after that comment, I looked over at the waving man walking quickly in my direction from the resort. He was in his fifties, and heavyset, but still had a full head of dark brown hair, and brown eyes that seemed to twinkle when he smiled. Secretly, I thought he might make a great Santa when he got a few decades older. He was also our go-to security camera guy.

"Hey, Tom. How's the security business going?"

"Not bad, not bad. I got called out here to look at some faulty cameras and thought I might swing by your friend's place to see if she was still interested in a security system."

"Lark? Yeah, as far as I know she's still interested. You want her phone number?"

"If it wouldn't be too much trouble. I left the card with her phone number at home because I didn't know that I would be coming out here today, but Kenneth called in an emergency call."

"Because of the broken camera?" Interesting. I pulled up Lark's number and held out my phone so he could program it into his.

"Yeah, that and I guess some FBI bloke came in here and spotted a whole bunch of holes in the system that needed to be filled in. None of the staircases had cameras, some of the staff-only exits, that kind of thing. Just finished installing them and upgrading the system."

Interesting.

"So the camera that was down, it was just a coincidence?"

"Oh, no. The wire had been cut. Definitely not a coincidence. Pretty clean job, too. Knew what they were doing."

The murderer had cut the camera. And they must have taken the staircases, knowing that there were no cameras there. How proficient of them.

"You heard about the murder, then, since you knew about the camera?" Tom asked, frowning back at the resort.

"Yeah, you could say that. I have the FBI bloke in the car." We both waved at the angry face looking out of the passenger window. I smiled even wider when I saw his face. "He's a little high strung," I whispered, as if Nic could hear us.

"Is that what you're calling it?"

"Better than a giant stick up his butt."

Tom laughed. "Well, I need to give your friend a call and see if I can slip out there to look around for a quote. Let me know how it goes, and thanks for the lead!"

"Anytime, Tom. Anytime." I waved as he strolled back to his car before I slowly headed toward mine, smiling innocently at Nic's disgruntled look. I slowed until there was no way to miss that I was doing it on purpose. His eyes narrowed at me and I gave him a wink.

Focusing on him and doing anything I could to annoy him, I could hide from my problems. Henry's death. My business failure. My lack of security. All that could be pushed down as I teased and tortured Nic. But there was a small part of me that knew it was to avoid looking at my own problems. Nic was easy. My problems were hard.

Deep breath.

I had a mission. I couldn't fix Henry's death or the company, but I could do this. Convincing Julia to move here and drag the object of Lark's affection with her. That was what was important.

And not the handsome brooding man in the car. Nope. It didn't matter that his eyes reminded me of a starburst. Or that he made me feel like I'd won something every time I beat him in a verbal battle. Or that he had gotten me out of the worst of my funk.

Nope. Not at all. Well, I'd admit my hormones might've been interested, but my hormones weren't in charge. I wanted a sensitive man, who thought about others before himself. Who would never ignore me or take me for granted. That was not handsome, sexy, playboy Nic.

Giving him one last smug smile, I lost sight of him as I rounded the car to get to the driver's side. Slipping in, I started the car, doing my best to ignore Nic's glances. I was not going to feel bad. I had a mission.

"Let's start the tour of exotic Barrow Bay, California. The town has been here since the 1920s when it was settled as a fishing town. Fishing was the main business until the 60s when small boats stopped being able to keep up with the bigger rigs. It slowly went into decline until 2007 when Dorothy bought the land for the resort and built it, bringing new life to the town." I rattled off the facts absently, reverting to my teacher's pet mode.

"How long have you lived here?" Julia interrupted.

"For about five years. I came here as soon as I graduated college. This was my mother's hometown."

"That seems like an odd choice," Nic commented.

I bit my lip and looked away for a second before focusing back on driving. "It was."

Silence reigned in the car for a moment as I got lost in my thoughts. First my mother died and now Henry. Well, that wasn't entirely accurate. First my father left, then my mother died, and now, Henry was murdered. I was going through my parental figures pretty fast.

"Where does your mom live?" Logan asked.

I softened when I looked back at Logan's sweet face. "My mom died. About four years ago. She was sick for a long time."

"Did she live here with you?"

"Yes. We had a house over near my friend's barn." In the poor section of the town. My mother had refused to let me move her, even after I could afford to. I hated that house.

"Your friend has a barn?"

"Yep. She's a horse trainer. Do you like horses?" I knew the answer before I even asked as his whole face lit up. "She offers training for children, if you're interested," I told Julia, but her face was closed, and she looked away.

I knew that look. I was willing to bet they didn't have the money. I had seen it growing up on my mother's face too many times to forget.

"Anyway, the town was almost completely dead, down to maybe four hundred people who were either too stubborn or too old to leave when Dorothy came. I don't know what convinced her to stay, or even drew her here in the first place, but suddenly my mom was talking about how Benny was helping Dee find contractors."

"Benny, the chief?" Nic asked, contributing to the conversation again.

"Yes, at least for now. He's retiring at the end of the year."

"And the town has already replaced him? With someone from the outside?" Nic stated with slight horror.

I smiled, glancing into the rearview mirror to see Julia's return smile. "Working on it."

Nic took in the exchange but didn't say anything.

"Anyway, after the resort opened, we started getting more tourists and more tourism money and we started revitalizing Main Street." Which we had just reached because, well, it was a five-minute drive. "On your left, you'll see the indoor playground and hourly daycare, followed by the tourist shops and antique shops."

"Anything good in the shops?" Julia asked.

"Do you like Barrow Bay keychains?"

"No."

"California keychains?"

"Still no." She added a shake of her head for emphasis.

"Then, no." I moved on. "The yoga studio is pretty good if you like yoga." Another guilty look away. Yep, definitely money issues. "On your right you'll see our restaurants, starting with Andre's, our local Italian restaurant."

"Good food?" Nic asked.

"Entertaining food."

"That doesn't answer the question," he pointed out.

"Hmm, it doesn't?" It didn't, but it was going to drive him crazy if I didn't explain. "So next—"

"Is that the bakery that the man was talking about?" Logan pointed at Dough & Nuts, pressing his face close to the glass.

"Well, that is the best bakery in the area. We have people travel from towns around us for their donuts, and the nuts are amazing, too." I hesitated, risking a glance back at him before I went back to watching the road. "What man was talking about it?"

"The one with the missing hair."

We all tried to hold back our snort of laughter, being sensitive to all the bald men out there. But it was a close call for me.

"The missing hair?" That didn't leave many options. In fact, it only left Henry. Of course, there could be another bald vacationer.

"Yeah, he was talking to the lady about a cake. He said a bad word." The last part was whispered.

Nic turned around, giving Logan a gentle smile I wouldn't have believed he had in him a few days ago. "What bad word? I need to know for my bad word list." He smiled at Logan and winked, making my heart melt a little. Soft Nic was dangerous.

Logan nodded seriously. I guessed 'bad word lists' were a serious thing.

"Boobs," he whispered. "She said that it would have to be earlier because of the boobs and brunch. Right before the other man yelled at him."

We all had to bite back a laugh again at him saying boobs was a bad word. Julia took over and talked to him about what bad words were and why we didn't say them. I, on the other hand, couldn't stop thinking about what he said.

Yelled? He couldn't be talking about Dan? That would make the man with missing hair Henry for sure. What was the coincidence? I glanced at Nic, who looked back at me before he turned towards Logan.

"Do you know the man that yelled at him? I don't like people who yell."

"No." Logan shifted, a little uncomfortable with all the attention.

"And what did he say?" Nic tried to keep his voice calm, but it was starting to get more excited.

"That they had a problem that needed to be fixed. The man missing hair told him to go away. That he had everything under control."

Huh. That didn't sound like Dan after all. I was under the impression that Dan had been straight-up threatening. Could it be another bald man? Or did Henry get two threats in one night? The night before he was murdered. And was he threatened before or after he texted me?

"Anything else?"

"That he'd be sorry."

"Who said that? The man with hair or without?" Nic asked, softly. Gentle Nic was shocking. But he was good with Logan.

"With."

"Could you recognize him? If I showed you a picture? Or you heard a voice?"

Logan thought for a second. "No. I didn't see his face."

Yep. Someone threatened Henry before the murder. Two threats if you counted the threat that Henry's wife claimed happened.

"Should we call John?" This seemed like a good lead.

"No. I'll text him. It's hardly evidence." Nic picked up his phone with a sigh and started sending the message. "Good job, Logan. You did a great job telling me what you saw."

Logan blushed and looked away, but I caught a glimpse of a smile in the rearview mirror.

"Hmm. A full head of hair. That could be a few people. Could it have been Dan again?" I mean, Dan had already threatened Henry in public. It stood to reason that he could have followed him to do it again.

"Maybe. We confirmed that there was a blow-up in the lobby the night before. Charlotte was honest about that. But he doesn't seem like the type to do it a second time."

"Why was he here?" It wasn't like Barrow Bay was that common of a vacation spot.

"Dan? Or Henry?"

"Both, but that time I was questioning Dan."

"His brother is married to one of the girls who's a manager at the resort. I don't remember what position. He visits them frequently on the weekend."

"Huh. I would have thought I would know that."

"His brother's not very active in the town from our background on him."

"What a small world—"

"What's happening there?" Julia interrupted, pointing to the boarded-up coffee shop and the people grouped outside of it.

And when I said people, I meant Judy, our local real estate agent, and a man and woman that I couldn't get a clear view of.

Were they looking at the shop?

I glanced back at Logan, trying to decide if it would be rude to be nosy. He looked like he had told us everything. We could get distracted.

"I don't know, but I would love to find out," I answered, looking at Julia. "Want to experience some small town charm up close and personal?"

She grinned from ear to ear. She was *so* in. We were going to get along fabulously. I pulled into Miguel's parking lot, which was next door to what used to be Tops, and we got out, Nic sighing loudly. I thought he was trying to pretend that he didn't want to be nosy. Too bad we didn't care. Nor did I believe him. He was an FBI agent. Didn't that make him nosy by job definition?

"Judy," I called out. "Imagine seeing you here."

"Jen," she said cautiously. "What are you up to today?" She moved in front of her clients, her skirt suit swishing with the movement. She had on black heels, ones that I knew were comfortable since she was on her feet all day, even as her arthritis got worse. Not that she was old, maybe around forty at the oldest. Hispanic like her husband, John, her beautiful black hair wound into an updo that I was jealous of. My hair was too fine to stay in any hairdo that nice.

Despite her attempts to block me, I managed to confirm that one of her clients with her was Will, a bartender from The Pub.

Who was married.

To a drag queen...

Oh my god. I was so excited. *Breathe, Jen. Stay calm.* I'd never met a drag queen. No bouncing. I was pretty sure bouncing would scare them. I felt like I was meeting a celebrity. Had I known that this could happen, I would have looked into it more. Maybe watch some TV shows about drag queens. I felt underprepared. But Will had said that his husband would never leave the city.

"Just giving a tour to Julia, Logan, and Nic. Have you met them?" I sounded normal. I was pretty proud of myself.

She gave them all a welcoming smile. "Julia. Logan. How nice to see you again," she said in a normal voice. "Early," was hissed at me under her breath.

Oops. I forgot Operation Captain America was a secret. I wasn't supposed to drop off Logan and Julia into Judy's manipulative arms until later. I hoped Will could keep his mouth shut.

"And Nic. I haven't met you, but I've heard so much." Judy turned to smile warmly at Nic. Too warmly.

Nic's eyes widened and he went white.

This was so worth the stop. I was giddy.

"Why?" Nic blurted out. He looked good pale. It really brought out his eyes.

"Why?" Judy asked, looking at me in question before returning to him. "My husband is John. Hernandez? The detective?" She looked at me again and I raised my shoulders like I had no clue.

I completely had a clue, it was just more fun to make him paranoid about the town talking about him. So much fun.

"Yes. I know John. Jen didn't mention you were his wife." He shot me a scowl that should have made me feel bad.

It didn't. He would learn I had very little shame when it came to the town's antics.

"And who are you hiding?" I asked, moving past her, my eyes intent on the female next to Will. Will was over six feet, although not as tall as Nic, and had blue eyes that were even dreamier than Nic's hazel. Not that I was comparing or anything. Strong chin, blond hair and a fabulous sense of style, Will was a sexy beast. The woman… man—I was pretty sure that we were supposed to use the gender they were in at the time? So, I was going with woman for now—the woman next to him was even taller, equal to Nic's six-foot-six height with her hair. Her huge red wig was teased into the iconic southern 'big hair' and she had scarlet lips that I wish I could pull off. With light skin like mine, I stuck to browns and pinks. Reds washed me out. Her skin, however, was a creamy tan that hinted at Native American roots. The blue dress was skin-tight and revealed that she had a body that put mine to shame. No wonder Will married her. Him? No… definitely her. I would have, too. She was dazzling.

"Hello, Gorgeous. I'm Jasmine. What's your name?" Jasmine pushed forward and put her hand out for me to shake. I tried to return the gesture, but suddenly she grabbed both my hands, forcing me to spin before pushing me away to take in the whole look.

"I like Gorgeous. But if you insist, you can call me Jen," I answered, a little breathless from the spin.

"I love your shoes," she said

"I love your lipstick." I might have squealed. I claimed no knowledge of it, though.

"Your bag."

"Your hair." Okay, I might have gone a little fangirl on that one.

"Best friends?"

"Deal." I was pulled into a hug.

"What size shoe do you wear?" she asked, taking a longer, more envious look at my pumps, which were a white base with pink and black spots. One of my newer pairs, they went perfectly with my pink shirt and black slacks. I may not be gorgeous, but I was dressed to impress.

Not Nic. I had not dressed to impress Nic. I was pretty sure.

"Size eight."

"Damn. Oh, well. We will just have to go shopping together."

"I rarely go to the city," I confessed, my cheeks burning a little with embarrassment. I had become quite the recluse in the past few years. "But my best friend does on a regular basis."

"And does she shop?"

"Not at all. I don't think she has any shoes other than her work boots and tennies."

"Sacrilegious. We *must* fix that," Jasmine said, pressing her hand to her chest, just like Charlotte did, only I believed Jasmine. She really did think it was wrong. To be honest, so did I.

Judy was beaming like I had just made her money. It was a little off-putting. I looked over at Will and, well, he was staring at his significant other's assets. I don't know if he was even paying attention to the conversation.

"Yes!" I spun when I heard Gran's voice behind me. Gran was really Lark's grandmother, but when we became best friends, she adopted me. Which was good because she owned the local tea shop and I had tea needs. Gran was seventy-eight, even though she only looked and acted maybe sixty at the oldest. Her steel blue eyes twinkled at me as she told me her newest plan. "Lark needs new clothing. She has nothing but T-shirts and jeans. Nothing to tempt a man. You need to fix that, Jen. Soon."

"Lark isn't going shopping. You know that. That would take a miracle," I told Gran. Lark hated shopping with a passion she reserved for very few things. She had gone a few times with me when she had felt I needed a pick-me-up, but it took a pretty bad day for her to agree. "She'll insist that he should like her the way she is." And she was right. He should.

"I'm pretty sure he does," Julia volunteered.

"As well he should. But every girl should feel pretty when going out with her man." Gran peered around me to address Julia. "Julia. I didn't even see you there. Are you having fun on the tour, dear?"

Wow. Gran had already introduced herself to Brecken's family. I wondered if Lark and Brecken understood how far this had gone? Not that I was going to tell them.

"It's been interesting," Julia told her with a huge smile.

At least she was having fun.

"We just started," I interrupted before she told on me and my short tour detour. "And it's two blocks—do we really need to call it a tour?" I asked. Which was a mistake. I should have let her keep her attention on Julia. My bad.

"Shopping." Gran said before handing me a credit card. "Clothing. Real man-catching clothing. And shoes. And underwear." She leaned in and whispered too loudly. "Ones that he wants to tear off."

I looked around. Yep. Everyone heard that. *So amused.*

"Can I help? I'm good at man-catching clothing," Jasmine offered, with a wink.

"Who are you?" Gran asked, taking in Jasmine's whole appearance. After a second, her eyes went wide, and she leaned towards me. "Jen? Do you know that that's a man? What do I do? Is he a cross-dresser or transsexual?" Again. Too loudly.

"You mean transgender," I corrected quickly with an embarrassed look at Jasmine.

"So, he's going to switch?" She blinked at me innocently.

I was going to hell for wanting to laugh.

"NO. He... she... she's a drag queen, Gran. She also likes being a guy sometimes." That was the best I could explain it. Jasmine was pure awesomeness in a wig, in my opinion, but that wasn't a good explanation.

"Like the Dolly Parton people?"

It took me a minute to keep the laugh in, even with me biting my lips together for all I was worth. Out of all the common drag queen personas, Gran remembered Dolly Parton? I loved this woman.

"Yes, like the Dolly Parton people. Although personally, I do a better Cher," Jasmine answered.

"You can do Cher?" Gran asked, perking up at the mention of one of her favorite singers. "What about Aretha?"

"Oh, no, honey," Jasmine pulled Gran to her with a wink at the rest of us. "I would never dare to impugn the memory of the Queen."

Jasmine was in. Gran pulled up to her full height and nodded. She had been blessed. Gran took her singers very seriously.

"We have a sewing circle every Friday. You will be there. Bring cookies," Gran ordered.

"What if I make a better bundt cake?" Jasmine challenged. She was all sass. What were the odds that Will would move to a place where Jasmine belonged so well? He had to have known that we would love her.

I foresaw a whole new level of crazy coming to this town. I couldn't wait.

Gran smiled and nodded again. "I will pencil you in. Sallie Mae is supposed to be bringing the cake but that girl can't bake worth beans. Not that we tell her that." Gran turned and walked away. "Oh, and don't bother bringing anything but you and that cake," she said with a wink.

That was a lot of winking in a short amount of time. I held back my giggle. This was why I could never leave this town.

"Welcome to Barrow Bay, Jasmine. Do you want to sign the papers today?" Judy cut in, smiling like someone who had just gotten a huge commission. "Also, when will you two start looking at buying a house? I know the perfect home for two, only two streets back. By Jen's house, in fact." Judy pulled them away, pulling out paperwork, and went back into the building that used to be Tops. Will followed quickly, but Jasmine was moving slower.

Oh no. If I let them go without finding out for sure if they were going to be making coffee, Lark would kill me.

"Jas?" I called out. "You going to reopen the coffee shop?"

"Does a bear poop in the woods, child?" she called back, turning around to face me.

"So, that's a yes?" Unless the bear lived in a zoo. Not important.

"Only if people will pay for organic premium coffee sourced from my locations. Coffee is a religion."

"Lark will love you. I need to be there when she finds out you exist."

"I thought small towns hated minorities," Nic argued, obviously done with waiting for our conversation to be over.

We all turned to look at him.

"That is stereotyping, Nic," I reprimanded.

"She makes coffee," Judy said.

"And sings Cher," Julia pointed out.

"Frankly, we like her better than you," I added.

"Because she makes coffee and sings Cher?" He sounded hurt.

"And likes my clothing. Plus, she called me gorgeous. I love her. If Will wasn't prettier than me, I would totally make a play."

"Ah, honey, if I played for your team, I would take you up on that." Jasmine smiled at me as Will came back out to stand next to her, snorting at her joke.

"See? I love her." I pointed at her and smiled.

"And would you like me if I called you gorgeous?" Nic asked.

"No." Oops. Honesty was a little harsh right there. In fact, most of today. Nic didn't bring out the best in me. But I had to admit, the verbal sparring was fun, and I wasn't thinking about how horrible my life was. Surprisingly, I hadn't thought about my issues in a while.

"I'm still confused," he stated, with a flat look at me.

"Okay, pretty boy." Jasmine took over. She pointed at him. "You are a player. Girl in every city. Your compliments are surface and lip service. You want her to like you? Actions."

"I don't—" He tried to protest, but she ignored him.

"Like Will. He tried all the normal ways to get my attention. Gifts. Compliments. Always being around." Jasmine threw Will a glance that said there was more to that story, especially since Will was blushing. "But none of that worked. I'd learned a long time ago that words are meaningless. Gifts are fleeting. But actions? They show the truth." Jasmine touched Will's face, lost in her memory. "It was a review of one of my shows. In a major newspaper, for the first time. And it was *so* bad. Will paid off the paperboy. Asked the paper to take it down. Tried to distract me so I didn't look. And all without telling me. It was futile, but it proved he cared. And I never looked at anyone else ever again."

I melted. That was so romantic. I wanted that. That, right there. I was reactivating my account immediately. Or whatever it was called when I started using it again. I was pretty sure I still paid for it.

Nic rolled his eyes and walked toward Miguel's.

Oh. Maybe after I lose the FBI tail.

"Isn't he a charmer?" Jasmine commented.

"Been counting on his good looks for too long," I told her.

"No kidding. Don't worry, honey. He likes you." Jasmine fluttered her ridiculously long lashes at me in a wink.

"I don't like him," I protested. Badly. I didn't even believe me.

"Uh huh. Just keep calling him on his bullshit."

"I really don't. I want something else," I repeated my protest with more confidence.

"What?" she asked.

Well. I hadn't expected that question. The only thing that came to mind was boring. No, loyal didn't have to be boring. Or normal. Or reliable. Or steady. Okay. I could see why my subconscious was going with boring.

"Love?" Not a man slut I would have to chase around to make sure he wasn't cheating. Though now that I thought about it, maybe I had decided Nic was a flirt before I got to know him. He hadn't flirted with Julia, who was adorable. Or really, any female I had seen around him. Just me. Oh. I didn't know if I was ready to deal with that thought.

"Love comes in many forms."

"I wouldn't know." Yeah, no one could miss the bitter note in that one.

"Hmm. Don't worry. If he doesn't do it for you, we can figure that out, too."

CHAPTER 9

Nic lead the way to Miguel's, sighing dramatically when I didn't walk fast enough. Which again, made me slow down even more, Julia slowing Logan down with me. She fit in well, but Nic didn't seem to be learning. The more frustrated he looked, the slower I got. Frustrating him was one of the few consistently fun things in my life right then.

I smiled at him as we strolled, Nic waiting with the heavy, thick wooden door held open with apparent ease, although I had caught him try to pull it open twice. The orange wood door gave way to a festive interior, the beige walls nicely offsetting the blue and yellow busy tile on the floor and bar.

Miguel, a Hispanic man in his late fifties, who rocked board shorts and a Hawaiian t-shirt everyday, came rushing over, cutting off the hostess and sending her back to the podium.

"Jen! Love of my life! When will you marry me and make me the richest restaurant owner in Barrow Bay?"

"When your wife lets you." We hugged, but I pulled back faster than normal. "But I'm guessing you need some help?"

"Yes. Might you have time to look into my books sometime soon? The bookkeeper I hired didn't bookkeep, so much as take my money." Miguel's eyes didn't meet mine as he admitted that he had been duped.

I grimaced because I knew that he had hired his niece's friend to be the bookkeeper, a move I had not recommended. I was not one for mixing family and business. Firing someone was hard. Firing a family member or family friend was harder. "Not a problem, Miguel. I can find time next week." Since I probably wouldn't have a business anymore.

"Do you do everyone's books?" Nic asked.

I wanted to snap back that it was none of his business, but a glance at him left me questioning if he was actually curious. Not making fun of me or trying to insult me. But actually curious about what I did around town.

"As many as I can." A lot of people in town weren't making much of a profit. Sometimes saving them that little bit, especially around the holidays made a difference. And it made me feel good to know that I was helping other people.

"Jen is the best," Miguel told him. "Very few people as sweet or kind."

I blushed as Nic looked over at me, his eyes scanning mine.

"So I've been told," he murmured, before Miguel lead us to a table.

As I sat, I rummaged around in my purse, looking for a card. I knew I had thrown a few in here... There.

"Miguel? Here. Call Nina and she'll do your books for a low price. I'll vouch for her. She's good. After I fix them, at least." She'd never take my call again if I dumped them on her without cleaning them up. Not if I was referring another reduced rate customer. But she was the best bookkeeper I knew, and I wouldn't be happy doing it day in and day out. Every once in a while to help people out was fun. Every day was monotonous.

"Thank you, Jen." He leaned over and kissed my cheek before giving my hand a last squeeze and leaving.

"The people here really love you," Nic observed.

"I like helping them. I'm used to only making what seems like a small difference to my clients. Here I make a big difference to some of these people," I told him quietly, making sure no one else could hear us. Then I smiled. "It's not hard. You just have to be nice."

"And slightly crazy." He smiled in appreciation of our joking.

"Now you're catching on!" I grined, daring him to continue. "Then again, we've seen the same crazy in you." I couldn't help smiling even wider.

"What's sad, is that I'm starting to get that. This town is making sense. I've been here too long."

"Oh, honey, you've only been here four days, total. If we've corrupted you that easily, you had issues to begin with."

He snorted with laughter, which I didn't expect, but made me happier than I was going to admit.

"You may be right. You just may be right." He picked up the menu and started to read, his lips still slightly curled in amusement.

Samantha, the lunchtime waitress, had just walked up when a man came through the doors, drawing everyone's attention. The man's shirt was buttoned wrong, making the ends askew, and he hunched slightly, his eyes squinting at the crowd as he scanned the room.

"I know he's in here." He aggressively pushed past the hostess, who fell back before darting toward the kitchen in fear. Miguel tried to stop him, but the man saw his quarry and rushed toward us. Julia went white and grabbed her son, wrapping her arms around him and pulling them both into a tight ball, but not fleeing the table like I was debating. I hesitated, realizing that wasn't a normal reaction, but I turned to confront the intruder before I could ask about it. Nic got there quicker, though, and had already cut him off from being able to access our table.

"What do you want, Ellis?" Nic had gotten to his feet and moved to the front of the table, blocking Ellis, although Nic seemed to be the man's goal.

"You know him?" I got the question out right before Ellis started yelling.

"You are railroading him!" The man sputtered and I could smell the alcohol on his breath. Or maybe it was his pores. Either way, we were all recoiling slightly from him. Well, Nic and I did. Julia couldn't recoil anymore that she already had. "He didn't do it."

"Ellis, you need to talk to Dan about this." Nic was calm and steady, trying to use his voice to calm the man down, but the alcohol made Ellis bold.

"No! I saw Lindsey's article. You're all blaming Dan. He didn't inside-trade and he didn't murder that lying bastard."

Hey! I took in a sharp breath at this new insult to my partner, but Nic's glance told me to keep my response to myself. This must've been Dan's brother, the one that had a wife who worked at the resort.

Hold up. That would give all three of them the access to know that Henry would be there and probably access to the rooms because I can't imagine it's hard to get a key card if you work there. It would mean they also had access to the cameras.

"I can't talk about an ongoing case, but if you have any questions about the murder, John's heading the investigation, you can—"

"He's just as bad as you!" Ellis moved closer to Nic, who held firm, but I could see his muscles tightening. "All you lawmen, out to destroy the working man on the orders of the rich! Dan didn't do it. You are just focusing on him because he's one of the smaller accounts. I mean, yeah, he might have threatened Henry a little the night before. And the letters he sent to Henry telling him to stop lying." Ellis tilted sideways slightly before catching his balance. "But he didn't mean that he would actually kill him."

Well. His brother wasn't helping Dan's case at all. How *had* Dan become a client? After Nic's comment yesterday, I looked up the information on our shared system, but all that really told me was that Dan had been a client for three years, mostly simple stuff working with

Frank. Nothing that would have attracted him to our firm.

Was it possible that he was our client because he was involved? Instead of the other way around?

"What letters?" Nic asked, snagging a chair and pulling it closer to them. Ellis was swaying more than a drunk man should. It wouldn't be long before he passed out.

"The letters he sent to the office. Henry replied saying that everything would be fine. That Dan just had to keep silent."

Shit. My head dropped to the table and I debated hitting it a few times. I couldn't believe Dan's brother just said that. This was why lawyers told everyone to never speak to the cops. I was sure Ellis was trying to help, but he just made it worse for Dan and Henry.

I also really needed to admit that Henry was compliant in covering this up. Not just absent-minded and busy. I mean, I knew it, but I hadn't really admitted it to myself. That statement destroyed what little hope I had. I was probably reaching, thinking that Frank was acting in Henry's stead.

"He swore!" Ellis was back to yelling, but the effort was throwing him more and more off balance. "That man said that the special projects would be fine, so long as everyone kept their mouths shut."

At this, my head popped back up. "Special projects?"

"He swore!" Ellis listed again, before he started to drop. Nic swung him into the chair as his eyes closed. "He swore—"

"I heard. You just rest." Nic waited until Ellis's eyes were closed before he looked at me. "Is this town always this exciting, or is it just me?"

"It's definitely you. You're trouble. I knew it the moment I saw you."

"Sure. I'm sure that's what you were thinking." His smile told me enough to know what he was insinuating.

"Shush and call John. I'm sure that our little blabbermouth over there needs some time in confinement." I gave Ellis an unhappy look, then watched as Nic moved away to make the phone call. Miguel intercepted him, both of them talking in low tones that I couldn't overhear. All of the other staff had cleared out, obviously smarter than we had been.

"Okay, what was that about? The whole story," Julia demanded, her arms still wrapped around her son. "I know it's involving the dead guy."

"Short story, my business partner was covering up for insider trading for two gentleman, whom one is his brother." I pointed to where Ellis was snoring with a wince. Nic was talking with two men near the door, both dressed in Barrow Bay police uniforms, but I couldn't see who it was. As we watched they came in, propping Ellis up on their shoulders and with a quick nod, they took him out the door.

"Yeah, I got that. And?"

"It's not really appropriate for little ears."

"He's the nephew of a cop. He's heard worse. Spill it."

"Well, my partner was murdered at the hotel yesterday, and Dan is suspect number one. After this, maybe higher than one?"

"Are they going to arrest him?"

"Not that I know off. But they wouldn't tell me." I sighed. "And my business is going down, all because of *special projects*." I spit out the last two words in disgust.

"What are special projects?"

"I have no idea." But after this? I was going to find out.

Starting with Donald. The piece to this puzzle that didn't fit.

CHAPTER 10

By one o'clock, I dropped Julia and Logan at the hotel and into Judy's waiting arms for their tour of the house across from Lark's. Nic took one look at Judy and stayed in the car. I didn't blame him. Judy's grin took a notably wolfish tone when she looked at him. He was being stalked. Like a gazelle. And I was having too much fun making sure he knew it.

"Are you going to get out?" I asked, looking at him without moving my hands from the wheel.

"No." He didn't look at me. Coward.

"You sure? Looks like Judy's waiting for you." Yeah, I was a horrible person. I was okay with it.

"No."

"I feel bad. She's clearly waiting." She wasn't, but I had a feeling he wasn't going to check.

"She shouldn't be. Drive." He gestured toward the road. Still not looking at me or where Judy had been standing.

Hmm. Should I take him to my house where his car should be, like a nice person? Nah.

I drove to Lark's house, a cute classic cottage that was ancient. I think it was built when they founded the

142

town, and she loved it. I couldn't see why. The newer construction was just as cute, with half the issues.

"Why are we here?" Nic asked, looking at her house.

"Because kidnapping is how Lark made her man fall madly in love with her and I'm under orders to try it, too." Straight face. Keep a straight face.

His face turned white.

I locked the doors.

Yep. That was panic. I should probably be insulted, but it was too hard not to laugh. He was an FBI agent. He should be able to remember that he could just unlock it from the inside. Unlike me.

"Let me out," he said, glaring at me.

"Sure." I unlocked the door. He looked at me. Then the door. Then me. I smiled. "Aren't you going to get out?" Innocent. Nice and innocent.

"What's your angle?"

"Torturing you," I answered, honestly. And by doing so, forgetting my own problems.

"You know kidnapping is a federal offense."

"Is it?" Blink. Blink. I was so innocent angels would've been jealous.

"I'm getting out."

"Okay." I wasn't stopping him.

He looked at the door again, suspiciously. Too suspiciously.

"You have brothers, don't you?" I couldn't hold back my laughter anymore.

"Yes."

Ha! He expected me to lock the door as soon as he went for it. Please. I wouldn't. Maybe. I had to admit that the idea had some merit.

"I may be pathetic, but I don't need to kidnap a man," I told him the truth, instead.

"Why do you think you're pathetic?" He looked over at me, surprised.

I gave him a flat look. "Please. You took one look around my home and decided to try and seduce me. Probably after you saw all the dating books. You think I'm pathetic and desperate."

His jaw dropped.

Huh. That looked pretty convincing. Was I wrong?

"I didn't. Well, I did decide to flirt with you, but it wasn't... I didn't... I'm not sure that..." He stopped with a heavy sigh. "This isn't making me sound any better."

At least he realized it. I smiled at his bitter tone. "I'm picking up Lark for High Tea. You don't have to come."

"Yes. I do." His tone was even more bitter.

"Orders?" I asked, trying to hide my laugh. I didn't do it well.

"That's where Carrie wants to meet us."

"Carrie?"

"The woman you talked with earlier. When you wouldn't come out of your car."

"Ahh. How did she know where we were going? Why does she want to meet us?"

"Closing up the insider trading investigation."

"What? You guys are done?" There was a good point to this day, and I had found it. Other than meeting an actual, real live drag queen.

"Well, the team is. I get to stay to close up the murder investigation." He muttered with a grimace.

"You sound bitter."

He returned my flat look from earlier. "I'm being set up."

"Yes, you are. Why fight it?" Since we were being honest and everything.

"Because I like being an FBI agent."

"Do you?" I really wanted to know that answer. Could he be like me and be questioning his career choice? "Do you really like your job? Or do you just think you should?"

That earned me a full glare. Then a sigh. He looked away and studied the street for a few minutes before he turned back. "Yes. No. Some days. It is all I can ever remember wanting to be."

"And now?"

"Now? I love it, but... I have started to think there might be other things I like more."

"Like?"

He threw me a sharp glance, one that felt more important than I could understand. "Just...more."

I had no idea what to say to 'more.' "I hate my job. Well, that's not completely right. I like doing it, but everything that comes with it... I hate it. I hate dealing with over-egoed CEOs that think they know more than me because of a title. Or even worse, their minions, who don't trust me because I'm a woman, or an accountant, or whatever other flaw they found that day. I hate that I have no life because I'm constantly working. I don't even have the time to go grocery shopping, so I end up eating Chinese all the time, because we live in a small town and they were the only people I could bribe into delivering to me. And now I'm fat, single, pathetic, and going on a date tonight with *Donald Watts*." Mostly so I could pump him for information, but the point still stood.

"You could say no to the date with Donald," he pointed out.

"No, I couldn't. Dorothy picked him out for me. *Donald*." I shuddered. "I even hate the name. That's who they think I should be with. A Donald."

"Okay, one—there is nothing wrong with the name Donald. I think you just don't like this one. And two— you can say no. Like right now. Call Dorothy up and say no. You are not a victim."

"No. I will just go on the date and then break it to Dorothy very softly that I'm uninterested," I told him. Plus, I really wanted to know how he knew Frank. It was annoying me, and I had to ask someone. Donald was the least creepy of the two options.

"Why?"

"Because that's the polite thing to do."

"But what about—" He cut himself off with a click as his teeth slammed shut.

"What about what?"

"Nothing," he snapped.

I looked away as my phone buzzed. Jumping on the excuse to avoid the topic, I opened the text message.

Lark: *Is there a reason you are parked in front of my house? With Wolverine?*

I laughed slightly. Lark was horrible with remembering names, so she tended to give people nicknames. When we met, she called me Coco Chanel for weeks. I kind of missed it.

Me: *I have decided he's Cyclops.*

Lark: *Ouch. That whiny?*

Me: *Yes.*

Lark: *Hmm, Cyclops would be a better match for you, anyway.*

Me: *Excuse me?*

Lark: *Seriously. You love the classic hero. The do-gooder. The person who always put others above themselves.*

Okay, she might've had a point.

Me: *Maybe.*

Lark: *There you go. Has he made a move?*

Maybe? But there was no way I was admitting that.

Me: *No. He's investigating me.*

"Do you want me to make a move?"

Shit.

I looked up at Nic, who was clearly looking over my shoulder reading my text messages.

"No. No reading my phone," I cried, holding the phone to my chest.

"But it just got interesting."

"No," I repeated, waving him away. "No, you don't just read people's text messages. It's rude."

"But how else was I going to know that you like the classic hero type? Which I am, evidently." His smirk was so large they could have poured gravy on it and called it a country fried steak.

"No. No way, not happening, *nyet*, negatory, never, not really, no thanks, we're nixing that idea, nope, negative, nay, no siree—"

"Ok, stop with the English lesson. Why do you do that?"

I sighed. I really didn't want to explain all my stress responses right now.

Me: *Please come out here and rescue me.*

Lark: *On my way.*

I watched as Lark came out, locking the door behind her. Her natural golden-brown hair gleamed in the sunlight, nothing like my fake dyed blonde, and I sighed in jealousy. Lark was tall, thin, gorgeous and had the confidence of someone that everyone naturally loved. Not that she wasn't weird, because she was. She just didn't let it get to her.

"Hey. How are you two doing today? Also, before I forget, thanks for sending the security guy over. I need to get on that," she said, getting in the back seat. "Think we can talk Gran into making me some coffee when we get there?"

"I dare you to ask," I replied.

"Ha. You *are* Jen. Just wanted to check because normally you're at home working at this time of day."

"We were searching her house," Nic said with a shrug.

NUMBER'S UP
        149

"Again?" Lark's eyes widened, and she turned to me, waiting for an explanation. "And she isn't there protecting her records like a guard dog?"

"I have nothing to hide," I told her.

"You didn't last time, too, but you still tried to guard them," she reminded me.

I narrowed my eyes at them both at the memory. She was right, last time that didn't stop me from trying to protect my customers. Just in case I had missed something. These last three weeks must have taken more out of me than I thought. Or it was Henry's death. Or all of it. Whatever. The FBI could have anything they wanted. "I have nothing to hide."

"What about your underwear drawer?" Lark asked with a smirk.

"Pish. Not even that. I actually shop for cute underwear, unlike some people." I gave her a pointed look.

"Really? Tell me more…" Nic said, leaning into me.

"No." Not going to happen, buddy. He had his government-mandated chance to snoop, although I kind of liked that he didn't.

"Too bad." His eyes unfocused and his lips curled up into a smile.

I glared over where he leaned towards me, his arm on the console between us. "Don't mention my underwear." Or think about it.

"Really?" His smile didn't waver.

He wasn't properly scared of me.

"Really. Do I need to find more words to—"

"Please don't." He held a hand up to hold me off, leaning back into his side of the car.

"We're going to High Tea, right?" Lark interrupted. "Maybe we should head out?"

"Sure. Nic's friend's meeting us there."

"Nic has friends?" Lark quipped from the backseat.

"My co-worker," he corrected over his shoulder.

"Ahh…" she said, with a gloating smile.

Which made him realize what she said. "Wait. I have friends. Lots of them," he defended himself before throwing his hands up in the air. "You know what? No, I don't. I have the people I work with and… my brothers."

"You hesitated a long time before you said brothers," I pointed out.

"They're assholes," he muttered. "I love them, but they're assholes."

"Well, Dorothy would want me to mention that people who move to this town tend to gain lots of friends quickly." I couldn't help but gloat. Yes, I was a horrible person, but I just couldn't stop myself.

"Like the woman we—"

I glared, and he cut himself off. Yeah, he almost let the chicken out of the bag on that one. I drove off quickly, jumping to the first subject I could think of that wasn't Julia.

"Do we have any suspects in Henry's murder?"

"No." He looked at me like I was crazy.

Yes, I realized we had just talked about this. *Go with it.*

"Who would you go after?" He asked after a second.

"Tony," I said confidently. "I would go after Tony. He is the only one who had any reason to kill him. Plus, he tried to kill a horse. That shows he has no morals."

"He's in San Francisco out on bail. I checked in with the local police. No chance of him being out here."

"Well, there went the obvious. Dan? He's in town, we have witnesses that say he threatened Henry the night before. He's a solid candidate. Plus, usually the guilty are the ones screaming 'railroading' without any accusations."

"Lindsey made some," Lark told me, showing me her phone. "Evidently, she couldn't find out where he was during the murder. And she confirmed the threats and had pulled a quote from someone back in the city that said he had been acting weird recently and meeting with unsavory characters."

"Interesting," I murmured before Nic frowned at me.

"What about some of Henry's other clients? Are there any others that have ties to the area?" Nic adjusted his sleeve as he asked, a clear sign he didn't want to talk about Dan. Why?

"I don't know about them. I told you, I only stuck to mine. I didn't even know Dan had any ties." I decided to let Nic have his change in topic and ask about the other loose end that was bothering me. "What about good old fake Scarlett? From the emails?"

"We've got nothing on that either. We tracked the account but couldn't find anything." Nic sighed and leaned back in his chair. "I have no idea what the weather has to do with any of this. Even if the weather was hotter than it really was."

"They were trading *incorrect* weather reports?"

"Yes."

"That's even weirder." I sat for a second and thought.

"What about his son?" Nic asked, glancing at me.

"Frank?" Lark asked from the back seat. I was glad she did, because for a second I thought Nic was talking about Dan's son. I had no idea if he had one or not.

"Yeah. He doesn't have the best alibi," I told her.

"Sucks to be him."

"Not really. Henry had a lot of money. Frank is probably set for life," I responded.

"Wow. That's cold," Lark told me, and a glance in the rearview mirror told me it came with a concerned look. "What brought that out?"

"He smiled at me." I still wanted to punch him a little for being that callous.

"Wow. That bastard. We should string him up by his toes." She was mocking me, but she might be right.

"Today," I clarified. "He tried to get me to keep the business open with him taking over all of Henry's cases until we found a new CPA from the approved candidates he had."

"And he was smiling?" Lark asked with a frown.

"See what I mean?" I threw her a look. "It's not okay. My business partner died yesterday, practically in front of me. I saw the body. I might be fully embracing denial, but it still hurts. Excuse me if continuing a business that is already struggling and going to be completely ruined when the news of his murder breaks in a real newspaper, pulling my reputation down with it, and is only going to attract—" dishonest clients. Was that what he was talking about with special projects? *Shit.* It had to be him. The insider trading had to be him. Why would Henry take the blame for his *son's* crimes?

Oh, Henry.

He *had* always been a better person than people around him deserved. But now I was conflicted. Should I tell the FBI of my suspicions? Henry went to great lengths to protect his son. Were my suspicions a reason to negate that?

"Again, with the thoughtful silence," Nic complained. "What are you thinking?"

I looked at him, with what I'm sure was a guilty expression before I looked away. "Nothing." If Henry was covering for Frank, then Frank had no reason to kill him. Unless Frank thought Henry might flip? No, Henry wouldn't. He was loyal to a fault. As this proved.

"Don't 'nothing' me. You've had that expression several times and yet you won't share the thought. It's frustrating."

"What will you give me for it?" Did that really just come out of my mouth? I checked Lark's expression in the rearview mirror and her mouth was dropped as low as mine wanted to be. Correction. As low as Nic's was. Was that too flirty? Aggressive? I didn't know what was wrong with me.

He tried a few times to come back from that one. "What do you want?"

"Why don't you think it was Dan?"

"Why do you think I don't?"

"Oh, please. He is the most obvious suspect and you haven't locked him up or even questioned him, despite Ellis saying you're railroading him. Lindsey would have reported that. And when I bring him up, you change the subject."

"He will be locked up, don't worry about it," Nic waved away my comment.

"So, he's guilty of insider trading." I knew that, but I repeated it anyway. Facts were always applicable.

"Yes."

"But not of the murder." I licked my lips as I thought.

"I didn't say that." His brow arched and he looked out the window.

"You didn't *not* say it," I pointed out.

He swung his head back to give me a good glare.

"I don't think you were supposed to point that out." Lark added unhelpfully from the backseat.

"Oh look, we're here!" Nic said, overplaying his excitement pointing toward the building in front of us.

I watched Lark's eyes narrow on him in the rearview mirror.

"You're a tea person, aren't you?"

"Why do I get the idea that it's a bad thing?" He asked, his eyes jumping from her to me.

"No. Liking tea is cultured," I answered.

"Unnatural," Lark countered.

"Sophisticated."

"Psychotic."

"Healthy."

"Coffee has just as many benefits," Lark exclaimed from the back seat.

"Oh, really? You sure about that?" I asked her, starting to warm up to our normal argument.

"Again. Look. There's a parking spot. Right. There. Please let me out of the crazy-mobile." That had both of us glaring at Nic, who glared back. "Also, I've been hanging out with you two too long if your conversations are starting to make sense. And that worries me."

I guess he didn't like our crazy. Sucked to be him because we were fabulous. My shoes told me so. I pulled into the space he indicated and turned off the car, rolling my eyes at how quickly he jumped out.

"Should we tell him that the whole town is probably here today?" Lark asked.

"Nope. Let him find out on his own."

"Wait." She pulled me back for a second. "You okay? No, that was a stupid question. Of course you're not okay. You still functioning?"

"I'm functioning." Barely. "Nic is a good distraction."

"Hmm, his butt isn't too bad. But I don't know if right now is a good time to get into a new relationship." She gave his butt a good studying, though.

I did too. Just to make sure it was still as good as I remembered. It was.

"I'm not. I'm helping him get away from the town's manipulations."

"You sure? Because that doesn't sound like you. You're more likely to help the town." She gave me a hard stare. "And *we* are here. Getting away from the town's manipulations would not be bringing him here."

"He wasn't supposed to come."

"Why did he?"

"His supervisor made him."

"Really?"

"She's awesome. She ripped into him earlier, too. I like her."

"So, let me get this straight. The FBI is searching your home for evidence for insider trading—"

"Which they won't find since all *my* customers are clean."

"—but Henry's weren't, I'm assuming, —"

"No." I admitted with a disappointed sigh. "Well… what if I think it might have been another person who did it, but Henry is —was— taking the blame because he wanted to protect them?"

"You think Frank did it." Lark rolled her eyes at me.

And she complained about me eye rolling. Also, was it that obvious?

"Maybe. Should I tell them? I mean, Frank might have done the crime. Helped with the crime." I corrected. "He should be the one punished, right?"

"I don't even understand what a CPA has to do with insider trading. I just know it does," she admitted.

Good point. Lark might not have been the best person to ask about this.

"Are you two coming?" Nic yelled out the door. I could see the woman from earlier inside talking to him as soon as he turned back toward the tea house.

"We'll be right there," Lark called back, putting her hand on my arm to stop me from escaping. "No, seriously. Are you okay?"

"No. But I'm functioning. And quitting. My job. I'm quitting my job." I hadn't said it out loud yet. Not in a complete phrase like that. Not that it was correct. I wasn't really quitting so much as... it didn't matter. I was no longer going to be... me.

Hello chest pain, my old friend.

Then again, I hadn't panicked since... when I got out of my car before I met Nic. When we walked into the resort together before Henry's death. Well, excluding Henry's death, but anyone would have an issue with that.

Huh. Did that mean that my anxiety quieted down around Nic? I wondered why.

Scratch that. I didn't want to know that answer. I couldn't keep Nic. Despite the town's attempts.

Lark's face loomed in front of me as she searched my eyes for the truth.

"I got drunk last night. There may have been a little crying. A lot of cake and romantic movies. Happy drunk Jen watched some things I'm not proud of." Like teen movies. "I'm processing my grief. I'm... keeping moving," I admitted.

"Why didn't you call me?" she demanded.

"I texted. And because I needed to cry ugly tears and you would have tried to make me feel better. Then it would have gotten crazy because your antics are crazy, and I was happy drunk Jen, and then I wouldn't have cried my ugly tears." I wasn't sure that even made sense.

"Okay then." She turned and faced the Tea House. "Seriously though, you think they might break the rules and bring me coffee?"

"Are you going to bring them Brecken, wrapped up with a Barrow Bay Police Department badge on him?"

"Nope."

"Then no. I'm guessing no coffee for you."

"He went on a case, I think undercover, and I haven't heard from him in a while." Lark admitted, looking away, before her eyes flickered back. "Like, a long while."

Huh. Well, a good friend would break confidence and tell her his family was here to move in and bring him with them, but I was pretty sure that would freak her out more.

"He'll call," I said, instead.

"Sure. I mean, it's cool if he doesn't. I will just tell everyone it's his fault." She pressed her lips together for a second. "I just don't need Lindsey to know."

"Would I ever tell Lindsey anything?"

"Yes." She glared. "If it was good enough gossip, you would tell her everything."

Damn. She was right.

"This isn't good enough." I assured her, and she looked relieved. "Now, can we go in and get this over with?"

"Remind me again… Why aren't they making *you* make Nic stay? Why am I the only one with the magic relationship draw?"

"Because I'm going out on a date with *Donald Watts.*" Wow. I had met the man for five minutes, and I couldn't hold back how much I disliked him. He might've been taking the brunt of my hatred of my life. And be a little creepy. Maybe a combo.

"How did Lindsey not know this?" Lark pulled out her phone and started scrolling. "Nope. Nothing. I'm texting her. I'm so disappointed."

"You do and I will kill you and make it look like an accident," I told her as I set off into the Tea House. After she accused me of telling Lindsey everything.

"Please. You have no more defensive skills than I do." She followed, hooking her arm into mine.

"I don't need defensive skills. One well-timed honk at that monster you keep trying to convince me is a horse and it will be all over."

"My daughter's mare and I have come to an agreement. I let her attack people trying to kill me and she doesn't try to kill me anymore."

"You disturb me."

She shrugged. "I'm a horse trainer. We're flexible." She winced. "That didn't sound right."

"Yeah, that sounded a little dirty," I teased, as we walked in the door.

"Lark! Sweetie. How's Brecken?" Lark's Aunt Helen came forward to greet us, giving both of us a quick hug. Helen was in her fifties and ran the Tea House for Gran, who was supposed to be retired.

I tried to hold in my snickering because Lark hadn't been kidding. They really had put the pressure on.

"I don't know. You should ask him," Lark said, rolling her eyes.

"Helen. It is so nice to see you again," I interrupted before we could go down the Brecken path. I had heard the conversations and they were not pretty.

Helen blinked at me. "It's been two days."

Okay, so I was doing it badly. Sue me.

"Dorothy made reservations?" I asked to distract her, this time more effectively.

"Yes, and then this nice lady called to make them for four. Have you met Carrie?" She turned to Carrie with a smile. "She was just telling me how you met Nic." She turned to me and whispered, "I approve. He's a hunk-a-hunk-a-burning-love."

Again, very loudly. We really needed to have a discussion about whispering in this town. Also, they hadn't approved a few weeks ago, so I was confused. What had changed? Were they really that desperate for someone at the resort that Dorothy had called in reinforcements? Last time he was here, Gran gave Nic an epic setdown. He had come inside and tried to bring me in for questioning, but Gran had told him that no one, not even the police, could interrupt High Tea in this town. Given that Brecken and John hadn't even bothered to get out of the car, Gran had won.

I heard a snort from behind me where Lark was standing, and Nic was smirking proudly at me.

"Dorothy said he would be the perfect fit for her resort," I threw him under the bus.

"Oh, it's not just the resort," Carrie added cheerfully. "She needs a head of security for all the properties in California. The job would just be based here."

"Et tu, Brutus?" Nic muttered at her.

"Et tu, Brute." I corrected, because, well, I couldn't help myself. And his glare was so sexy. I was getting a lot of that kind of sexy right then. I snickered. People really needed to get that quote right.

"A position here? At our hotel? So, Jen wouldn't be dating men from out of town anymore?" Helen asked, her face breaking out into a smile.

Wait… me? When did I get involved in this? Where did this run away from me?

"Nope," Carrie answered, still grinning from ear to ear.

"He would get to stay and no more online dating," Helen followed the thought out.

I had so many questions… Which to ask?

"How did you know I was dating online?" I demanded from Helen, while glaring at Lark, who was suspiciously looking at a tea display. She only drank coffee. I wasn't buying that she suddenly was interested in tea.

"Lindsey posted an article about it," she answered grinning as she held up her phone, showing me the blog.

I needed better ire.

"I hate Lindsey," I muttered under my breath. Mostly because I vaguely remembered talking about my plans at The Pub when she was in hearing distance.

"So, tell me more about yourself, Nic. Nicholas Kelly, right? Good Irish name. Are you Irish?" Helen asked pulling him deeper into the Tea House.

Carrie stood watching me with a huge smile on her face.

"You set him up," I accused her. And after we got all honest with each other this morning.

"He likes you."

"You want him to quit?" I was confused. I thought she liked lateral transfers.

"He needs a change." She was quite proud of herself, standing there gloating at me.

"I thought you were a fan of just finding a new challenge."

"I am. Here is his new challenge. And yours." She walked over to me and smiled even brighter. "Are you up to it?" She threw the words at me before she turned and walked away.

My chin dropped.

"So... you still going on your date with Donald?" Lark asked, coming up beside me.

"But... Dorothy... what just happened?" I couldn't anymore. I had lost control somewhere, and I didn't know where to go back and find it.

"You've been Barrow Bay'd." Lark nodded, as she confided her nonsense.

"Did you turn the name of the town into a verb?" She was so not helpful.

"Yep. And I have no shame about it. Sorry, not sorry." She followed the group in, leaving me standing in the entryway, staring after them.

Huh. This was what being bamboozled felt like. I was so confused.

CHAPTER 11

It took about a minute for me to become uncomfortable standing in the entryway by myself. People were moving around me, some going in for High Tea, some heading toward the tea shop that was attached to my left. It took me another minute to gain enough confidence to follow the people who were clearly out to control my life. Slowly. Very slowly. Just in case I found the answer to avoiding their manipulations between here and the table.

Carrie was the first one to see me following and, knowing what I now knew, I thought her friendliness took on a decidedly smug turn.

"Jen. Come here. We saved you a seat." Between her and Nic.

I glared at Lark, who mouthed 'sorry' from her seat across the table. Traitor.

Yeah, I was soooo not telling her about Julia.

I sat.

"Why are you here?" I asked Carrie. "What—"

"Do you know what kind of tea you want with your service?" Helen asked, eyeing Nic with a smile.

"Vanilla Ceylon," Nic muttered.

I shot him a sharp look. That was my tea. The one that Lark brought me this morning. How did he…?

He saw my look and sighed. "My brother's wife. She was pregnant and screamed for eight months about not drinking her teas. She had read somewhere that it could be bad for the baby, and so she went cold turkey. It was hard on everyone around. We all got to know our teas after that."

"He's been ordering from us for a year. Ships them directly to his brother's house," Helen told me, beaming with pride at him. I was pretty sure she would have adopted him if she could.

"You knew about the Tea House?" Lark asked, her eyes huge.

"You buy teas. And send them to your sister-in-law," I clarified. How was that not something we knew?

He shrugged and looked away.

"One of our best customers. He found us on our web page maybe a year ago," Helen beamed at him. "He stopped in the other day to say hello and to buy some more to bring home in his suitcase."

It was official. Barrow Bay loved him.

"I didn't know you guys shipped." Lark gaped at her aunt.

Nic flashed Aunt Helen a smooth smile. "All the way to New York where my brother and his wife live."

"But what about the High Tea when you came here?" This couldn't be happening. He was FBI Nic. Asshat Nic. Satan. Not some tea-buying, murder-solving man who pushed me into a wall and tried to protect me with his own body. Was I wrong about him? No, I knew I was wrong about him, or at least my first impressions. But *how* wrong?

"She didn't know that he was *Nic*. Tea Nic," Helen shot him a fond smile and gave him a half hug.

He shrugged. "I got a free cup of chamomile tea out of it."

Oh, god. He actually really liked tea. He hadn't been trying to make fun of my tea the first time we met. He'd been really curious. And I was way too defensive. I had been very, very wrong.

"They are going to have you married before you leave," I warned him under my breath.

"They are trying to match you up with me. That threat rebounded on you," he replied just as quietly.

Damn. He was right.

How could I stop this? Or at least slow it to a reasonable, healthy speed? Or I could go for broke. Charlotte might have been right about the transparency and all that jazz.

"We're not getting married," I told Helen.

"Of course not, dear. It's too soon for that. He hasn't taken the job yet." She patted me on the head before moving toward the kitchen to get our tea.

Also, I was pretty sure no one else ordered. Or did I miss that?

"She didn't take my order," Lark commented.

"You were going to ask for coffee," I pointed out. "She knew it. You knew it."

"Did not," Lark argued.

"I knew it," Nic volunteered before shaking his head. "It's too late. I'm on the inside of the inside jokes." He leaned back rubbing his face.

"She knew better than to ask you, Lark," I added, ignoring his muttering.

"She didn't ask Carrie, either," Lark pointed out.

"I already made my choice before you three got here," Carrie told her. "Since I was, you know, on time."

Oops. My bad.

"They were in the car, flirting," Lark told her.

"Were not," we both said simultaneously.

Carrie sighed and looked at Lark. "They're so cute."

"I would agree, but I'm slightly scared that she might kill me. She already has a plan," Lark admitted.

"I would never," I exclaimed. Maybe a little too loudly. Everyone in the Tea House was looking at me.

Never mind. I *might* kill her, after all.

I sank lower in my chair. "Can we get to the point?"

"Fine. Tony Harris wouldn't talk, but Dan Ellson was willing to work out a deal with the prosecution to plead guilty in return for turning in his sources. He is heading back to the city now to make his statement. Henry already admitted to his part before his death, so we are going to consider that to be closed. Thank you for your help in this matter," Carrie spoke quickly, covering everything in a smile.

"But— why—?" I think I missed something?

"Nic will stay a few more days to close out the murder investigation—"

"And get sold to the highest bidder," Lark interrupted, with a smirk at Nic and me.

"I'm not for sale," Nic snapped, flashing her a scowl.

"Oh, of course not, sweetie," Helen soothed, as she dropped pots of tea at our table. "We don't sell people for money around here."

"Nope, just for a good job and two cows," Lark muttered.

"Give it up with the cows, Lark. No one is paying two cows for your broke ass," Helen yelled over her shoulder, as she buzzed around the room, waiting on tables and bringing items. Lark made a face at her before looking at her tea with disgust.

"Lark, you know that coffee is just hot water run over beans. Almost the same thing as tea," I was trying to keep my laugher down at the look on her face.

"Sacrilegious. You only get away with this because the coffee can't hear you," she hissed. I wasn't kidding. I was worried she would turn and start whispering about her precious.

"We need to get you away from the coffee more," I told her, seriously concerned at her coffee addiction level. Were there coffee rehabilitation centers? I would have to look.

"Not happening unless you want to die," Lark muttered back.

"Just ignore her," I told Carrie, who was watching both of us with a huge smile on her face. Glad she was having so much fun. "She hasn't learned not to threaten people in front of law enforcement. Brecken's trying to break her of that habit, but she just doesn't seem to get it."

Carrie turned to Nic, who looked somewhere between shocked and amused. "If you don't move here and take the job, I am. These people are fantastic." She took a sip of her tea. "And make a really good tea."

He nodded. "Yeah, I have been Francine's favorite ever since I found this place." He sighed, his shoulders dropping as the air left his chest. "I'm moving here, aren't I?" He sipped his drink, but his eyes looked resigned. He was defeated. By tea?

Wait... what? How did that even make sense? Who makes those kinds of decisions over tea?

"Good, we already started processing your paperwork. You're free after this case ends," Carrie told him, cheerfully.

He was just... and he did it over tea?

"No." Everyone turned to me before I realized that I was the one who'd spoken. "Um... no. Nope. Not this way. This isn't how it works. Normal people don't do... this. There are decisions and... pros and cons and... debates and... mental anguish. You don't just go to tea and decide 'well, these people are fun. Maybe I will stay.'" Things were changing too fast.

"Why not?" Carrie asked me.

"Because... because... because, no." He couldn't do that. People couldn't move here like that. There had to be debates!

"I thought she was more eloquent than this." Carrie watched me with amused eyes.

"She normally is. I think we short-circuited her," Nic said, now laughing at me.

"This is not a laughing matter," I glared at him. "You are not moving to Barrow Bay. I say no. Nay. Never. Nyet." He needed to get away from our crazy to weigh the decision properly. He would thank me later. We had obviously been a bad influence and he was making rash decisions. People never liked the results of rash decisions. Yes, he would appreciate this when he was being logical again.

"Is your permission required?" Nic asked, with a smile. "Also, you're going into other languages. I think it's time to call the synonym lesson for today."

"Nope, you don't need Jen's approval at all," Helen said, as she walked past, dropping off tea cakes. "Welcome to the town, Nic. I will have Judy give you a call as soon as she is done."

"*Twilight Zone*. Have we joined the cast of the *Twilight Zone* and no one told me?" My world was spinning worse than yesterday. Maybe it was a combination effect? Or maybe a leftover hangover symptom?

"I already checked. It never filmed here," Lark told me over the table.

She would know.

And just like that, I hit my limit.

"Done. I'm done for the day. Finished. Spent." I got up, gathered my purse and looked at Carrie. "Are you done with my house?"

"Yes."

"Good. I'm done."

"I got that impression," she replied, taking a cucumber sandwich and biting into it. The little ones, that were cut into a triangle that I only found at High Tea. She just ate it. Like them being done invading my house and office wasn't an issue. That my possible implication into the crime wasn't an issue. Like I wasn't an issue.

I don't know why it upset me. I *wasn't* an issue. I mean, I knew there wasn't anything to find. I didn't do anything wrong. In fact, I was the one that reported the issue to them, but right now, being treated like a non-issue was... devastating. I was an issue, damn it. I was important. They should care what I do.

"I'm important." The thought broke free of my mouth without the precursor thoughts, and I was too embarrassed to explain, so I turned and took a step to escape. No. I spun back around. "No one moves to Barrow Bay on a whim. *No one.* That is not how things are done. Hear me? *No one.*" I spun back and left. Well, I got all the way to the entrance before I remembered my tea. I loved that tea. It was physically hurting me to leave the tea. But my pride had limits.

"Here you go, sweetie. Continue your dramatic exit," Helen said, handing me a tea in a to-go cup. Fitting. That was how my day started, too.

"Thank you, Helen."

"No problem, sweetie. We can talk about the wedding colors at a later date."

I said "thank you" too early. I should have known better.

CHAPTER 12

It only took me a few minutes to get home, and I was still stunned that the house looked exactly like it had before I left that morning. Nothing out of place. Well, okay, not too far out of place. Some of my books were moved around, but only someone as detail-obsessed as me would notice.

I collapsed onto my couch and turned on the TV, searching until I found my favorite show. I settled in, ready to ignore the world. Ignore that my source of security was gone. Ignore that my partner was dead. And... okay, I was out of things. But they were big things. I still couldn't grasp that Henry would never again call to tell me about a new opportunity or complain about his newest client. Never again. Life was too short. So were my TV episodes.

At five p.m. my phone buzzed.

Unknown: *Hello Jen, this is Donald. Are we still on for today?*

Oh, no. I still had my date. Well, my date-slash-unknowing interview. I needed to find out what the special projects were.

To be honest with myself, I was regretting not canceling. Nic had told me to, several times. Why didn't I listen? Oh, yeah. Because Dorothy asked me to. And there was a small part of me that wanted my impression of Donald to be wrong. Okay, a very small piece, but still a little bit of me thought maybe Dorothy could have found my Brecken. My Prince Charming.

Hah. Donald was no one's Prince Charming. And to make matters worse, the phrase made me think of Nic. It was his schtick. Charming, disarming, and effective. I bet he was a great FBI agent. But, was he really going to stay? In Barrow Bay? I mean, no one really just decided to stay like that.

Well, John and Judy did.

And Lark.

And we were working on Brecken. Hmm. Maybe they did. What did that mean for me?

Which led to a different question: Did he like me? I mean, really like me, outside of all the bantering because of the case. Or, was it just the chase, the challenge? If I gave in, would he lose interest? Was that really a thing, or was it just in movies?

I had no idea.

Donald: *Jen? Does six pm work for you?*

No. Yes. No. Panic. I couldn't tell him no this late. That would be rude. Plus, then I would have to ask Frank my questions.

Me: *Yes. See you then.*

I could go out with him for one night. It was for Henry. Or at least, his case. I just had to keep that in mind. I was going to find out how he knew Frank and what the special projects were.

I looked at my phone. Was I that curious? Yes. I *was* that curious, even before I added in Henry's murder. I needed to know.

Shoot. I needed to get changed, because if I went on a date to The Pub in what I was currently wearing, Lindsey would write a blog post about it, and not a complimentary one.

At five forty-five I was ready and heading out the door, dressed in a cute skirt and my sheer heels with sparkles on them. They made me feel sexy. Strong. A Cinderella going to the ball ready to find her Prince.

Which they had failed to do, so I was getting a new set of heels after tonight.

Something sexier.

Maybe less Cinderella and more Marilyn Monroe. I could be more like her.

Yep. After tonight, I was retiring Cinderella. I wasn't waiting for my prince to come find me with the perfect pair of heels. No, I was going to go find him.

I hesitated as my mind brought me a picture of Nic grinning at me.

He had been written off soon after the first time he opened his mouth. I still kind of had him in the no chance category. Was I wrong? Could he stay? And want a family? And be loyal? *Was* he my Cyclops? Was I his Jean Grey? Wait. I wasn't sure they ended well.

Also, I needed to limit Lark's control of our movies. I was drawing the line at Marvel life references. This had gone too far.

***

I made it to the bar at six and slipped in, nodding at Joe, who was working the bar. Will must have been at home with Jasmine. Lucky man.

The bar was what I imagined an English pub to be. There was even a picture of the Queen in the corner. And Prince William and his family. But not Prince Charles. Joe was still angry over his split with Princess Diana. Another thing in this town that I had learned not to ask about the hard way.

Glancing around, I saw Donald in one of the booth seats along the wall with an empty glass in front of him. He saw me and waved, standing slightly and reminding me of how short he was. Not that I cared about height. That would make me superficial. And I wasn't. Much. I didn't even focus on the receding hairline or the pudgy belly. Nope. I wasn't thinking about his weight. That would make me a hypocrite. I faked a smile and waved back.

"Jen. So glad that you came out tonight." He really did seem to be happy about it. His smile beamed, as he stood and lead me to his table, which was nice. I couldn't remember the last time a guy stood when I walked over, much less met me in front of the table. Maybe I wasn't giving him enough credit. My smile warmed up.

"I'm glad you asked me out. I could use the distraction." Well, his grandmother asked me out, but I could overlook that. Probably.

"I'm truly sorry about your business partner. Were you close?" He gave me what I could only assume was his best sad face. It was superficial, the sad face people give when they knew someone was hurting but didn't feel the pain, themselves. After Frank's lack of sympathy in our earlier conversation, I appreciated the effort.

"Yes. He hired me straight out of college. He was more like a father than my own." Not that beating out my father was an achievement.

"He was a really good guy."

"You knew him?" How? Although I had consulted on some things for Dorothy, Watts Enterprises was not a customer. In fact, as far as I knew, Henry had no contact with anyone from her family company at all.

"We had done some business together," Donald said stiffly, lifting the menu and glancing at the options. "We worked on some special projects for my own personal finances."

Special projects. There it was. The phrase I was curious about. I buried my head in my menu, trying to hide my internal debate. Should I just ask? I mean, he offered the information. I didn't know why it would be weird to ask about it.

"Special projects? Funny, Henry hadn't told me anything about it."

"Henry was keeping it quiet for me. Nothing important." He waved his hands as if he were throwing away the conversation. "But I know a lot about you. He talked about you frequently."

"Did he?" Because that would be even more weird. Henry didn't talk about me much to his clients. Just like I didn't talk about him to mine unless there was a reason. What reason would he have? Unless this was a lie.

"Yes, although he forgot to tell me how beautiful you were," Donald replied, leaning closer trying to gaze into my eyes.

I looked at my menu. Yep. That level of corny indicated he was lying. The points he had earned by the greeting had been cancelled out. I glanced up to catch Becky's eyes, and she hurried over.

"Is that how you met Frank?" I asked, turning back to face Donald.

"Frank?" Donald recoiled slightly, trying to cover it by leaning back in his booth. "I… yes, that's how. Well, not exactly. We met at the club."

"The club?"

"It's not important."

I was pretty sure it was. "So, you guys are personal friends?"

Donald picked up his glass, drinking down the last bit before looking at me again. "Sure. He was the one that recommended your firm."

Funny how Henry never told me that. And he would have. "And you guys met at the club. What a small world." How did I ask about the club without seeming suspicious? Maybe—

"Welcome to The Pub. What can I get you?" Becky asked professionally as she stopped at the table, smiling at us.

"Why does everyone say it like that?" Donald asked her, jumping on the change of subject. She looked at me and I smiled at him.

"No reason." My answer was a hint for Becky. Donald wasn't the one. This was my signal that I wasn't happy and that I might need an out. The bigger the out, the better her tips. She nodded while getting her pad out. After the number of bad dates I'd had here, we had the system down. Not that we had any practice recently. I had been pretty good at dating before my last boyfriend, but after him I had only flirted when the opportunity arose and dated even less. In a town with very limited resources in eligible bachelors, it wasn't hard to be reclusive.

"Whatever. What are you getting?" Donald asked, although it edged into the demanding category.

"Hot wings and garlic fries." There was going to be no kissing. Not going to happen. That wasn't why I was here.

"You are one of those girls that don't mind eating in front of men." He eyed me up and down, hesitating at my stomach that he couldn't see around the tabletop. He must be focusing on what he remembered. "How novel. Most of the girls I eat with just pretend to eat. It's so annoying."

The words were all right, but his tone seemed to be judging *me* more than those poor girls he usually dated.

I was starting to get more superficial by the minute.

"I like the food here." Also, I needed some alcohol if I was going to last until the end of dinner. "And can you add a lemon drop?"

"Yes. And an old-fashioned." He looked at the menu again, his eyes flicking from item to item. "Are the steaks here good?" he asked, his face scrunched up as if he were debating the validity of her answer.

Becky glanced at me, her brow arching slightly before she smoothed it out. "Yes. We don't get many complaints on the menu." Yeah, he was making friends left and right over here.

"Then, I will have the steak. Medium rare. I like it bloody."

Becky glanced at me and I was pretty sure she was questioning my sanity. Hell, *I* was questioning my sanity. "He's Dorothy's grandson," I told her, so I could explain a little. It wasn't like I could admit that I wanted to pump him for more information about my dead partner and his son.

She smiled tightly at him before shooting me a look and returning to the kitchen to place our orders.

"You know, I was surprised when Henry asked me to come out this week," Donald said, putting his menu back in the holder at the head of the table.

"Henry asked you to come out this week?" I was stunned. Why? What was he up to?

"Yes. Even offered to pay for the room, even though I told him I would get it for free since I was family."

"I didn't know that the two of you were so close." That didn't compute. Henry was not generous. He argued over sending our clients Christmas cards. There was no way he would offer to pay for a small client's room. Plus, I hadn't seen Donald's name on any of our client lists. What had Henry been up to? And had it caused his death?

"I'm surprised he didn't tell you anything. Nothing at all?" He seemed to be scanning my face intently, looking for something. Since I had no idea what he was talking about, I doubted he found it. I was starting to feel like I wasn't the only one here to pump the other for information. And that was a little worrisome. Maybe I should've just told Nic or John my suspicions.

"Nothing. I had no idea you were a client," I answered honestly. "In fact, I probably shouldn't have accepted a date with you, if you are. Were. Maybe we should call it a night." I started to flag down Becky so I could get mine to go, but Donald grabbed my hand and pulled it down.

"No. I mean, no, we just ordered. You are closing the business with Henry's death, anyway. Why should we rush out now?"

I could think of a few reasons. "I don't think—"

"Grandmother would be so upset to think I let you leave so quickly," he reminded me.

I dropped, leaning back in the booth as I studied him. He had answers, and I was tempted to try to get them out of him. Why did my partner, who never left the city, suddenly take a trip to Barrow Bay? Why did he stay in an expensive suite? A treat he was saving to be a retirement gift to himself. And he invited his ex-wife, whom he hated. Donald Watts, a businessman who had lots of connections in the business world—at least I assumed from his family's contacts alone—was saying that Henry had invited him too. Even though I had no idea he was one of our clients. And after doing all of this, Henry ended up murdered.

I was starting to get a better idea as to why. But I really hoped it wasn't true.

"You must be very busy with Watts Enterprises. What made you take Henry up on his offer?" I asked, accepting my drink from Becky with a smile and a murmured, "Thanks." Donald let her put his drink down in front of him, without acknowledging her at all.

Ass.

He studied the room for a second before taking a large sip and turning back to me. "He was right. I needed a vacation. Now seemed like the perfect time."

Really? The beginning of October was his perfect time for a vacation? Did he really expect me to buy that?

"Most people come in the summer. When it's warmer and you can swim," I mumbled, afraid if I talked louder it would come out accusatory.

"I visit then, as well. I spend a lot of time out here, trying to learn the business. Kenneth and I will be taking it over from Grandmother at the end of the year." He finished the drink and signaled Becky for another. Joe saw it and lifted a brow at me before starting it and handing it to Becky, who also was eyeing him. I hadn't thought to ask Becky if she had seen him here before.

"Really?" Huh. I knew Dorothy had been talking about hiring one of her relatives, but I had gotten the impression they were more… experienced that the man in front of me. At least one had been. I was willing to bet that Donald was the other candidate. The one she was going to deny.

"Yes. She should be making the announcement soon. I will finally get a real position," he sneered and took another sip from his new drink.

"I thought you worked for Watts Enterprises." Which was an important company. Important enough that he would have contact with most of the major players in the area.

He waved away my comment. "They don't actually let me do anything. I just sit in meetings and act important. My father doesn't trust me with any real work. That's why—" He cut himself off abruptly. "You're very easy to talk to, do you know that?" His words were a little slurring, but he'd only had one drink, so he couldn't be that bad. Right? I looked up at Becky, who was still watching Donald. Catching her eye, I mouthed, "How many?" She lifted three fingers.

Great. He was drunk.

"What will you be doing at the hotel?"

"OM. That means—"

"Operations Manager." I dealt with upper management on a regular basis. I knew the lingo.

"Ahh, I forgot that I was on a date with a smart girl. You're a smart girl, right?"

What answer did he expect? No? Yes? Eat dirt? I admitted I liked the last option.

I started to get up again, signaling to Becky to wrap mine to go. This wasn't worth it. I could just tell Nic and let the FBI figure it out. If I hurried, I could make it home before the fries were cold. Maybe. "Well, this has been nice, but I really think that—"

"What time is it?"

Not late enough. "Six…" I checked my phone. "Thirty." Wow. I don't know that I have ever ended a date this quickly. This might be a new low. Stellar.

He nodded. "Perfect. See you around." He took another drink, picked up his phone and began texting.

That was it? A 'What time is it?' and then 'Bye'? I got out before he could change his mind and pulled out my phone to text Lark, stopping by the bar to cancel my food and pay for my drink. The look on Joe's face when he said they hadn't placed the order yet told me what they thought of my date. And the chances of me making it to eating. I was not alone in my disgust.

Me: *How hard is it to switch teams?*

Lark: *I have no idea what you are talking about.*

Me: *Teams? Like, how do I become a lesbian? Is there, like, reverse shock treatment, or something?*

Lark: *How bad was the date? Also, that's still not how it works.*

Me: *Thirty minutes. He was drunk. What was Dorothy thinking?*

Lark: *He asked her to set it up. Told her he was too shy. I asked for you.*

Me: *Too rude, would be more like it.*

Lark: *Why didn't you say no?*

Me: *Because I'm stupid.*

And suspicious. I would call Nic and John in the morning with my new information. No point in covering for Frank.

Lark: *Wine?*

Me: *You have enough?*

Lark: *I can get more. Hailey is at the Tea House for their Princess party.*

Me: *Three bottles.*

Me: *Scratch that. Four. And bring something to watch. And eat. I left before I could get food.*

Lark: *Can I bring something Marvel?*

I sighed.

Me: *No. No Marvel movies. No romantic comedies.*

Lark: *So… unless you want to watch Disney movies I'm out of suggestions.*

I was out of better ideas and I didn't want to watch more reruns.

Me: *Disney sounds good. Let's do Disney.*

I was outside by this time, looking down the street. The liquor store was right there, only a few doors down. I changed directions.

Me: *I take it back. I will get the alcohol. You bring the movies. See you at my house in ten.*

Lark: *Deal.*

I crossed the street to the liquor store. Some days called for something stronger than wine.

CHAPTER 13

After spending too much money on enough alcohol for the both of us to drink ourselves into a stupor, I walked the two blocks to my home debating how overactive my imagination could be. I mean, it seemed too elaborate. Was Frank the real criminal, helping Tony and Dan commit insider trading behind Henry's back? Then Henry found out and admitted to the crime to protect Frank. Could Donald Watts confirm any or all of these theories? And why had Henry worked so hard to bring all of them here, in Barrow Bay, at the same time as the FBI investigation?

I was confused. And starting to think that Nic might be able to help me make it fit. Which worried me on another level. When did I depend on someone else to help me figure anything out?

"Jen," said Lark as she walked towards me with a bag that I hoped included something with lots of starch to absorb the alcohol. "What wine did you get?"

"Russian," I yelled back.

As we got closer, I could see her head drop to the side as she tried to figure out what that meant. "Please tell me you mean vodka."

"And Mexican varieties."

"And tequila? This is going to be a good night." She smiled and rubbed her hands together. "I texted Gran. Hailey can sleep over at her house, so I'm a free woman."

"Well, I don't plan on remembering much of it," I admitted. "By the way, thanks for the tea this morning."

"What do you mean?" She tilted her head slightly to the left. "What tea?"

Wait, if she didn't bring the tea this morning, then who... no. No, there was no way Nic did. Although he was there when I made it the first time we met. And he knew the Tea House. But he would have been really paying attention to me to—

"Nic brought you tea this morning and told you it was me, didn't he?" Lark bit her lip trying to hide her smile.

"No." That denial wasn't going to play. "Yes. Maybe."

She laughed. "He likes you *so* much."

"But he's mean to me."

"You're pretty mean back. Plus, some men are weird. Doesn't mean that he doesn't like you. Maybe he just didn't want to like you." She thought for a second. "In fact, he really just plays off you. I don't know that he's ever been the first one to be mean. Well, this trip. Unless you're about to spiral. Then he says something to get you out of it."

"You're crazy." And right. Could she be right? "Whatever. Let's go." Avoidance sounded good.

We both turned to walk up my walkway at the same time, which made it more awkward when we both stopped.

My door was open.

No. NO! No, no, no, no.

"Oh, hell," I moaned. Too many years being the person called in to handle the emergencies had trained me well, and it kicked in, keeping me from panicking. But it didn't stop me from staring at my alcohol with longing. My dream of avoidance was gone.

"Odds that the FBI left it open?" Lark asked.

"I was home after them."

"Want me to call John? I have him on speed dial." Lark gave me a sympathetic look while pulling out her phone.

"That's not normal," I told her.

"Yeah, but I have learned my lesson. I will never call 911 again." She shivered with the memory.

"You know, if you just stopped with the sarcasm you would be fine," I pointed out.

"You say that like it's possible," she answered. "Hey, John. Can you—" She suddenly glared at the phone like he could see her. "No. No, I have not found more body parts. That is not funny. No, really. Stop laughing." If looks could kill, the phone would be a goner.

"I feel the need to remind you two that this is about me, not you," I spoke up, hoping I would be loud enough to talk over John's laugher. When Lark continued to glare at her phone, I grabbed it and started talking. "John, someone broke into my house."

"What? Why?" He stopped laughing and got serious.

"I don't know. What do I do?"

"Wait there with Lark. No. Go to a neighbor's house and wait. Don't go inside. Nic and I will be there soon."

Why couldn't tonight just end?

"Jen? Lark? You girls okay?" Sallie Mae, retired teacher and certified gossip, walked by and drifted over to join us. "Jen, honey, your door is open."

"Yes."

"Is it supposed to be?"

"No."

"You had a break-in?"

"Looks like it." Screw it. I was drinking. I pulled out the vodka and took a swig.

"What is happening in this town? First Lark's body parts problem—"

"I don't have a body parts problem," Lark interrupted, only to be ignored.

"—then that awful murder up at the resort, and now a break in at your house. What is the world coming to?"

"Not to mention poor Bon, the horse that was murdered." Lark growled under her breath.

"I don't know. I'm sure it's nothing," I murmured, ignoring Lark, and keeping in mind that anything I said would go straight to Lindsey. More vodka. Hmm. Glad I spent the money and got the good stuff. Less burning when taking hits directly from the bottle. Score one for the vodka tasting sessions Lark dragged me to.

"Nothing? *Nothing*? This has to be connected. What would they be looking for?" Sallie Mae lifted up on her tippy toes, straining as if she might be able to answer her questions if she looked hard enough.

"You know, she's right," Lark said, slowly.

"You have a body parts problem?" I snapped. The alcohol was finally starting to kick in and my anxiety was less screaming and more giving a low murmur of "My life is ending."

"No, the murder and the break-in have to be connected," Lark said, ignoring my sarcasm.

"But the FBI has been through my entire house this morning. There is nothing there. Who is stupid enough to break into my house after the FBI leaves?" I rolled my eyes at the idea.

That stumped both of them.

"Jen, why was the FBI searching your house again? I thought you dealt with the whole insider trading thing. Wasn't that how the two of you got kidnapped?" Sallie Mae demanded.

Evidently, they had been stumped for different reasons. Hmm, probably should have waited to start drinking until after the gossip left.

"Because my business partner's son is a criminal," I said under my breath.

"The kidnapping wasn't related. That was because I have a big mouth and can't stand not knowing why I failed at being fabulous," Lark told her at the same time.

Oops. I shouldn't have said that out loud. I looked over at Sallie Mae. She was pulling out her phone. Yep. I don't know which comment she was going to text first, but I really would appreciate mine not making it.

"Please don't tell Lindsey," I asked, pulling out my best pleading face.

"But this is big," she told me. "Barrow Bay deserves to know."

Lark rolled her eyes at that, but I kept Sallie Mae's gaze, hoping the addition of my lower lip might sway her in my favor.

"Which?" I asked, hoping maybe Lark's big mouth would win.

"Both," she replied, before frowning at Lark. "Although, Lark having a big mouth isn't really anything new."

"I was being flippant. The truth is that it was my partner. The one that got shot. And he's dead, and I'm the only one left and I don't have a job anymore, and... and please don't tell her." I was ready to get on my knees. Or let her have my extremely expensive vodka. I was hoping she wouldn't take it that far.

"Fine. I need someone to take me to the sewing circle next month. Benny took my license."

"Yes. I will," I assured her.

And bless Benny for taking it, because she was a hazard on the road.

"You know, the only reason to break in would be because something changed from then to now," Lark said, still musing on my break-in issue. "Did anything change?"

I glared at her and then tilted my head at Sallie Mae. I wasn't getting into more trouble than I already was.

"Honestly, she has a devious criminal mind. Tell us," Lark encouraged.

Sallie Mae seemed proud of Lark's comments.

Crazy people. This town is full of crazy people. *Swig*.

"Three months. And I will keep your secret. Tell me." Sallie Mae offered with a shrewd smile.

"Two months. No more." She seemed pretty eager to know my issues. Negotiation seemed key.

"Deal. Tell me," she snapped.

"Well, after the FBI left, I came home and watched some movies. Cried a bit. Contemplated how"— pathetic I was. I edited that out— "this could have happened. Then I left for the worst date I've had in a while with Donald Watts."

"Dorothy's grandson? The worthless one? Why would you do that?" Sallie Mae asked.

Worthless? She set me up with the *worthless one*? Another swig.

"Because Dorothy asked," I told her.

She looked at me with her face scrunched up in confusion. "That doesn't make any sense. You are getting the hot new head of security. We picked him special for you. You two were so cute the last time he was here. She must have done it to make Nic jealous. Worked with Brecken."

I blinked.

Nope. I couldn't deal with that right now.

"How did you guys—"

"Nope," I cut Lark off. "We are not going to ask the why right now."

"Why not?" Lark whispered.

"Because I don't know that I can handle it. Moving on." Swig. Hmm. This bottle was going down fast.

"I don't think I can. I mean, how do they pick them? Is there a catalog somewhere with men who are looking for a change? Is there an Amazon-like site where they can post men who need a new life? Have they gone digital? Or maybe it's like a job posting? We have this job opening and this single girl... please apply here? I *need* to know," she whispered back.

I gave her a look that told her to keep her mouth shut.

"So, you went on a date? Must have been an early one since you're back already. It's not even seven. In my day we were out until nine at least," Sallie Mae commented.

"Horrible. He was drunk. Told me how he knew my partner, the one who died. It was weird because he kept asking if Henry had ever mentioned him. Which he hadn't. I didn't know Donald was a customer at all, or I would have never gone on a date with him."

"Donald asked Dorothy to set it up," Lark told Sallie Mae.

"So, the worthless grandson asked to be set up on the date and you're still home by seven?" Sallie Mae asked.

She was a great-grandmother. I was being judged by a great-grandmother. And coming up on the side of pathetic. I took another swig.

"I started to make my excuses, then he asked what time it was. When I told him, he said, 'Perfect,' and told me goodbye. After I had to listen to him try to explain to me what an Operations Manager is. Seriously. And the comments about how I'm smart. It was painful."

"So, he set you up to not be in your house tonight, and let you leave after he asked the time?" Sallie Mae looked thoughtful as she waited for my response.

"What?" I asked. She sounded like she knew something. Which shouldn't be possible. I mean, she was like eighty. Shouldn't I be more in the know?

I looked down at the bottle. I was out-cooled by a woman with no driver's license, twice in a minute. I should probably stop drinking.

"Well, I had a friend back in the day. She got set up like that by a couple of con artists. One would ask a girl out on a date and the other would rob the girl's house while they were out."

"But Donald has more money than I do," I protested.

"What else could they want?" Lark asked.

"I don't know. I want to think that it's about Henry's case, but I don't have anything. And if I did, I would have given it to the FBI this morning," I snapped.

"Well, that's good to know," a deep voice came from behind me.

I jumped and screamed. "Seriously? You snuck up on someone who just had their house broken into?" I swung around and gave Nic the evil eye. "Also, where is your car?" Because there was no way I missed it driving up. I was far from sober, but I wasn't that drunk.

"I walked. I was getting dinner." He looked at the house, escaping eye contact.

Hmm, could he have been trying to spy on my date? Because that would be cute.

Or... that might count as stalking. Was stalking allowed to be cute? Was I supporting negative stereotypes by thinking his actions were adorable? Stop. Not important.

Also, that had to be a drunk deduction jump. There were a lot of reasons he could be in town. Dinner, being the biggest. Since he said it, and everything.

"Someone broke into my house," I told him, still glaring.

"I see that." He studied the front door before swinging his gaze back to me. "Any idea why?"

"No." I had started to sound whiny. Time to put away the vodka. But first, one more swig.

"We think they wanted something in relation to the case," Sallie Mae told him.

I committed to two months of driving for nothing. Lindsey would know before the hour was out since, apparently, Sallie Mae couldn't keep her mouth shut. I really was stupid. No more drunk negotiations. That was rule one of CPA negotiation class: No drinking and negotiating. I didn't know what I was thinking.

Although, now that I thought about it, there hadn't been that class in college. Or a rule. But there should've been.

"But we searched the house. What could you have that is worth breaking into your house to get?" he asked, studying the front door, which was half open, taunting me.

Hah. Good to know it wasn't just me. He was just as clueless.

"Maybe we should go in and look to make sure it wasn't just a normal break-in before we jump to conclusions?" I asked. Who knows, coincidences could happen.

"That seems like less fun," Sallie Mae muttered.

Great. Barrow Bay's own Jessica Fletcher. Before we knew it, we would be this generation's *Murder She Wrote*. I refused. That town was dangerous.

"When John and his team have cleared it," Nic said, laughing at Sallie Mae's complaints.

John pulled up at that moment, leading a team of three regular officers that I didn't recognize. Lark, however, waved hi to one.

"Hey, Zach," she yelled out. "Gran has more of your tea for you."

He turned white and walked quickly into the house, barely waiting for the cue.

We all looked over at her, and she shrugged, pretending not to know about the wide grin on her face.

"He pushed me out of a car to avoid Gran once. I don't forget those things."

Snorting, I looked back at my house, waiting for the all clear. It took a few minutes, but John came out and waved us forward.

The four of us walked up the walkway, Nic leading, followed by me, then Lark and finally Sallie Mae, who I had given up any chance of getting to leave. Again, I could hear the click of my shoes on the cement, but for the first time, I wasn't soothed by it. It was like they were mimicking the beating of my heart. Thump. Click. Thump. Click. Thump. Click.

"Maybe we shouldn't go in." Where did my alcohol go? Why did I put it away? Worse, I think I handed it and my food to Lark. Stupid idea.

Nic turned around. "It's all clear. No one's in there."

"What if my stuff is ruined? I don't know if I could take that tonight. I reached delicate flower levels of stress when I saw the door broken into."

"Delicate flower?" He gave me a clueless look.

"There are levels of how well I can take bad news. Most days I'm rolling with it. I'm good at rolling with it. I'm trained to roll with anything life throws at me and turn it around. Bad days, I shop. Today? Today if I take one more hit, I might break. Hence delicate flower."

"Okay." He scanned my face. "Do you want me to go look for you?"

"Yes." Then he could break it to me softly. While I drank myself into happy Jen. Where that girl went to, I didn't know.

He turned and went through the front door. I could hear him talking with John, but not what they were saying, and he came out looking grim. Too grim.

"No." I threw a hand up. "I don't want to hear it. Everything is trashed, isn't it? It wasn't enough that I'm losing my business and my business partner? Now I've lost my stuff, too?"

"Jen." Lark interrupted. "Yoga."

Breathe. She was reminding me to breathe. Because when my anxiety goes crazy, *I* go crazy. But I was better at handling it if I remembered to breathe. Or, at the very least, breathing kept me from passing out.

I could breathe. Breathing was easy. I could handle it if I just kept breathing.

"Okay. Tell me," I told him.

"You sure?" He scanned my face a little more before stepping closer and giving me a hug.

Oh, my. I let myself wilt into his arms, taking his comfort and wrapping myself into his warmth. It took me a few moments to notice how flat his stomach was, and how it was pressed against me, letting me feel his abs. Plural. I was getting a little dizzy from that thought. I could feel his hand rubbing my back, sending shivers down to my— well, maybe I should step away before this got more awkward in front of one of the town's biggest gossips.

My arms were going to let go any day now. Any day. And then I would pick my head up off his chest where it rested on a pectoral that was swoon-worthy. Which I was about to do. Swoon. A good reason to stay right where I was. Since swooning would be embarrassing.

Okay, I wasn't giving this up any time soon. Might as well just try the conversation.

"I can take it," I told him. Well, I told his shirt.

"The house was searched, but there is no damage, and nothing taken that we can see," he told me, quietly.

"What?" Well, that was good news. Why did he look so grim? I pulled my head away to get a better look.

"So, they were looking for something?" Lark asked.

"Was it something to do with the murder?" Sallie Mae added.

"We don't know," Nic said, pulling away enough that he could see my face as well. "What changed? What could you have that we might have missed?"

"I don't know." I scanned my memories. "There was nothing."

"There had to be something," Sallie Mae pointed out.

"If there was, I don't know what it is," I told Nic.

"We need to search your house again."

Great. "Where am I sleeping tonight, then?"

"With me," Lark volunteered.

No way. Never going to happen. I needed sleep.

"I will get a room at the resort," I said quickly. "No offense, Lark, but your cottage only has two bedrooms, and both you and Hailey snore."

She laughed. "We really do," she told Sallie Mae.

"Great!" Sallie Mae beamed at me.

I didn't know why she was so excited. My eyes narrowed. Irrational happiness from anyone in the Sewing Circle made me suspicious.

"Nic? Could you take her there?" Sallie Mae blinked up at him, her face hopeful.

"Um, I need to stay here—" Nic looked back at John, trying to gauge what they were doing.

"I mean, her house was just broken into. They could come after her next. She should be protected with a police escort."

"He's with the FBI, Sallie Mae," I pointed out. And after that, she was on her own. She didn't keep the secret, so I wasn't keeping my promise.

"Even better. The FBI is even better than the police, right?"

"I heard that," John called out from my doorway. "The FBI is *not* better than the police. We are the *bomb*."

"Bomb squad," Nic muttered.

"What was that, FBI boy?" John called out again. "Come and say it to my face."

"Okay then." I interrupted what I was sure would be a long discussion of the merits of traditional policing versus federal. "I think that I can make it to the resort by myself, but thank you for offering someone else to take me, Sallie Mae." Wow. Politeness took a weird turn there. I repeated it in my head checking for the drunk factor. Nope. That was right. Huh.

Sallie Mae shook her head and leaned close, like she was going to whisper, before speaking in normal tones. "But we brought him for you. You need to spend time with him to catch him. You're too old to believe in that magic pussy nonsense. Chemistry is mental, honey. And you have got to show him that the two of you have it."

Lark doubled over, laughing so hard she was having trouble standing up. I grabbed the food and alcohol out of her hands before she broke it. Nic was alternating between blushing and turning white, which would have been fascinating, if my mind wasn't trying to sort through everything that was just said. "Magic pu—" no. No, I couldn't go there. Not with someone old enough to be my grandmother. *Great-grandmother*. Just no. I couldn't believe she just said the p-word.

"What books have you been reading?" I had to, because, well, it had to be asked. I mean, I could think of a few candidates, but I was struggling to picture sweet, nosy, retired schoolteacher, Sallie Mae reading them. I needed a drink at that thought.

"I'm old, Jen. Not dead. I can read naughty books too," Sallie Mae replied, arching one brow at me as if challenging me to say anything.

No way. I was already regretting the picture of us reading the same books. Not that I read a lot of books. I gripped my alcohol tighter.

Right. Vodka. Tequila. Happy drunk.

"Lark…" I whispered. Maybe she could drive me to the resort. Without making any references to magic anything.

"You remember when I needed someone to come with me to Gran's dinner and you bailed? And Brecken ended up coming instead? And I somehow ended up being sold off as unconventional benefits?" Lark gleamed wickedly.

That girl had a memory like an elephant. How was it that she never remembered people's names?

Shit. "I can drive myself." I only had a few sips of the lemon drop before leaving. I would be fine to drive. I looked down. And half a bottle of straight vodka. Not so much.

"Escort," Sallie Mae said, glaring at Nic.

Nic looked to still be in shock from the way his mouth hung open and he glanced from person to person.

"Fine," I caved. "Nic, you're driving." I started walking toward my car, pulling my keys out of my purse.

"God, yes." Came the response from behind me before his body moved past mine in the rush to get to the driver's side door.

Maybe I could get started on more alcohol. I stopped and looked down at the bottle of vodka in my hands.

"Illegal, Jen." Lark called out from behind me, amusement clear in her voice. "Drinking in a car is illegal. Try not to do illegal things with the law next to you."

I was pretty sure she was right. Forgetting would have to wait.

CHAPTER 14

Closing the open bottle and throwing the bag in the trunk, I got in the passenger side, handing Nic my keys.

"This sucks." All I'd wanted was to get drunk with Lark. This was not the way I wanted to stay at the resort for the first time.

"The resort is actually pretty nice."

"That's not what I'm talking about."

"The date?"

"Are you being annoying on purpose?" I complained.

"No. Just trying to figure out how the date went without asking you. Directly," he admitted, glancing at me quickly to gauge my reaction before glancing back at the road.

"Do you like me?" Oh. Hmm. Maybe the vodka was a bad call because I was pretty sure that I was going to regret asking that tomorrow. Keeping mouth shut now. I was nice and fuzzy at this point, my anxiety buried in the glow of alcohol.

I looked over at the giant next to me.

He was so hot. Really hot. And a great hugger.

Damn. I need something to talk about.

"They brought you here for me. I thought that they thought Donald was my speed. Unimpressive, boring Donald. But no. They brought you." Wow. I had no control over my mouth.

"Are you disappointed?" he asked.

I thought he would smirk, or throw me a practiced grin, but the look I got was unsure. Unsure was weird on his face.

"With an Irish god in an FBI suit, is being disappointed even an option?" I admitted, deciding to just go with honesty. I didn't like that I made this man unsure. He shouldn't be unsure. Ever. That wasn't who he was. Or at least, who I thought he should be.

That got him to smirk. Good. I liked his smirk. Way too much.

"I can be an ass sometimes," he admitted.

"I think you're a sexy ass." Hold up. Too far. Was there a truth serum in the vodka? Because I knew that shouldn't have come out of my mouth. "You never answered."

"What? If I like you?"

"Yep." I watched him, my head rolling back against the seat. The way he moved as he drove. The way he glanced over at me as his face got serious. The way….

He pulled the car over. Hmm, this could be fun. Good thing the middle console was low. I could hop right on over it, even drunk. I had never tried to do it before, but for him, I could be game.

"Carrie's right. I do want to leave the FBI. In fact, I had already quit before I came here. This was to be my last assignment."

Hmm… not the kind of 'fun' I was hoping for. Probably for the best. I don't know how good I would be trying to maneuver the middle console in heels.

Wait. Did he just say he had *already quit*? Before he came here? Or did my drunk mind make that up?

"Okay." I definitely should have gotten water. Or eaten the food I had put in the trunk. Because I had found relaxed-drunk-Jen, and now I had a hot man telling me his deepest secrets.

"I have wanted to quit for a while. My family doesn't get it." He looked away, running his hand through his hair before resting both of them on the steering wheel, his arms braced. Gorgeous arms, with muscles popping….

Re-focusing to the serious conversation. Serious Jen was needed. Stupid vodka. Stupid break-in. Stupid… life.

"They keep telling me that this was my dream. That I should be happy. I mean, how many accountants get to work in forensic accounting for the FBI and be an active agent? I'm a sexy, *smart* James Bond. I *should* be happy."

"But you're not?" I could do this. No giggling. Or kissing him. This was not the time. This was serious. "Wait. *You're* the forensic accountant?" No wonder I'd never met them during the search.

"Nope, I was definitely not happy. Then I came here." He fell silent again, ignoring my question about being an accountant, and I was really hoping he wasn't waiting on me because I had only two responses and neither were appropriate. Plus, we were going back to the forensic accounting thing later. When I was sober. I had so many questions.

"John welcomed me to town. Judy gave me a listing of a house for rent by the month when I left the last time."

Rent by the month? That didn't sound like her. She liked to get people to buy homes. More commitment. Pin. Putting a pin in that. We would be going back to that, too.

"Like, to them it was a done deal. I was vetted and pre-approved. Like a car. Carrie even handed me my final paperwork today and Dorothy met me at the entrance to the resort with my new paperwork. And, to be honest, I only said yes to mess with you. I knew you wouldn't be able to handle it being decided on so flippantly. I wouldn't have been able to handle it. But... I said it and it felt right. Then Dorothy was there, paperwork in hand, and it still felt right. So, I did it." He smiled over at me and I returned it.

Hold on. I was pretty sure that wasn't the right reaction. My hormones were making it hard to tell. I squirmed in my seat before focusing on his eyes, no, lips, no. Hair line. Yep. Hair line. It wasn't sexy. Ish. Was I supposed to be smiling?

"I realized this fits. This town. This crazy. I'm happy. I have been happy since the day I knocked on your door and you were still in your pajamas. You didn't fit into my mold. It shook me. Challenged me. You teased me. Fired back at my lines with your own. Soon I was happy every time you called me on my shit. When I left, I went back to being unhappy. Then they offered to send me back to close out the case. And I found my it again."

Okay, so this just got even more serious.

"I'm drunk." And too honest.

He laughed. "Yeah, the rapid blinking clued me in."

Rapid... no, I was not getting distracted.

"You aren't staying for me, right?" For goodness sakes. I was such an idiot. "Oh, my god. I get it."

"Get what?"

"Get why Lark is not, *not* dating Brecken. Because it's too much. Too much pressure. What if it doesn't work out? Or if it's just enough. Just enough to not run, but no one's happy." Like her first marriage.

He still looked a little confused. "Am I going to be an ass if I direct this conversation back to me?"

"No. Yes. No... I think the answer is no. The point is you're not moving because of me. Right?"

"No. Yes. I mean, I don't know that I can fully remove you from part of the equation and say that the conclusion would be the same, but it's not all about you. It's about me. And my wants. I want you. Or what you represent. I want to get the girl. And have a home that I see more than a few times a month. And the community. And friends. Non-work friends. And I won't get any of that if I don't make a change. So, I'm making a change.

A change that everyone seems to think will be good for me. For the potential of getting what I want."

"I'm drunk." Oops. I was pretty sure that wasn't the right answer. "And that was complicated."

"That sounded like a no."

"No. It wasn't a no." I didn't think. "It was a request for clarification on the question." There was a question in there, right? It felt like there had been a question.

"Do you want to go out? With me?"

Finally. I knew that answer. "Yes."

"And you're okay if I move?"

"No. Yes. Maybe?" *Let's kiss and take it from there.* No. Don't say that.

"Mostly yes?" he asked, pushing for clarification.

"Don't you need to freak out about it? Stress out? Debate the pros and cons? Talk it over with your friends? Drive yourself crazy until you can't think anymore?"

He frowned. "Is that really your question? Right now? It's that?"

"That's what's confusing me," I admitted. "I can understand wanting to change. I get that sometimes we dream the wrong things will make us happy." Like money. "But... how do you just... move? Decide to move?" How did I decide to change?

He laughed.

"That's not the right answer," I informed him.

"I didn't. I have been thinking about this for awhile," he smiled broadly. "I was just waiting for... motivation."

Ooh. I think he meant me. I beamed. Well, I drunk-beamed, so it could be anything from smiling like a crazy person.

"Does that mean we can make out now?" I asked, my eyes fluttering to try to keep his face in focus.

"How drunk are you?"

"Very," I admitted.

"Nope. Sober making out only."

"I hate you." I glared. Maybe.

"I'm pretty sure you don't. Not one little bit." There was the smirk I loved.

Liked. The smirk I *liked*.

"No one likes a cocky man," I muttered.

"In my experience, lots of people do."

"*People*?"

"People like me." He got even smugger. I really needed to find a word for that.

I wasn't sure he understood what I was implying. Probably for the best. If he knew I was jealous it would feed his ego and then there really wouldn't be room in the car for both of us.

"You sure about that? Your boss seemed pretty excited to get rid of you."

"She just wants me to be happy," he said, pulling onto the road.

He was serious about the no drunk make-out sessions. That was very responsible. I had never been so disappointed.

I was contemplating the morality of making a move while drunk and the exact amount of time until I was sober again. It was okay. I'd heard making out in a car was uncomfortable, anyway.

"Nic?" I waited until he looked at me to confess. "I don't think Henry was working on Tony's accounts. I think it was Frank."

"So do we."

"And I think… hold up. What?"

"We've been through all your company's records. You think we wouldn't notice that the cover-up was clumsy, and Henry's skill is too high? But he confessed and all the records are under his name."

Well, I guess I was stressing over nothing.

"Then you know about Donald?"

He gave me a sharp glance. "Donald? Donald Watts?" His gaze went unfocused as his lips pursed to the side slightly.

"I don't have any proof," I said quickly. "But I think he's the source of the information for the trades."

"But it makes sense. And gets—" He cut himself off, giving me a sheepish grin. "Never mind."

"Oh please. We both think he is Tony and Dan's source for the insider trading. But did he have an alibi during Henry's murder?"

"We didn't ask. Why do you think Donald's involved?" He glanced over at me with a frown.

"Special projects." And being a creep, but I didn't think that would stand up in a court of law.

"Special projects?" Nic echoed. With the eyebrow thing. I really needed to tell him not to do that when I was drunk, and he was trying to be good. It made me want to do bad things. Very bad. Things I would do with him in… seven hours? Yeah, I should be sober again by then.

"Frank approached me today about continuing the business with him taking over his father's clients and some new ones with special projects."

"And that's suspicious?"

"Would you trust your business to us? After Henry got caught helping to hide insider trading?" I snorted. It wasn't sexy.

"No."

"Unless…" I drew out the word, leading him to the next logical conclusion.

"I was a criminal," he conceded.

"Ding, ding, ding. We have a winner."

"What does that have to do with Donald?"

"Tonight, he told me that he had worked with Henry."

His gaze came flying to me, his eyes open wide. "No. He didn't. His name wasn't on any of the records."

"That's what I thought, too. I don't date clients." Not that it had been an issue in the past. Most of our clients were married or old. Or female.

"So, they had worked together but there are no records."

"And Henry was after me all the time to get a bigger in with Dorothy's company. I would have heard about him working with Donald on anything." I was pretty sure.

"You think Frank worked with him without Henry's knowledge."

"Yep."

"Anything more than just guess work?"

Not really. Well, it was all guess work, but pretty strong, logical guess work. "Donald said that he was working with Henry on a special project."

"Ahh." He went back to focusing on the road while he thought. "Is special projects a term you guys use a lot?"

"No." No more than any other business. Or all of the ones we serviced. I was too drunk for this.

We reached the resort and Nic focused on parking before he turned to study me. "I need to go talk to John. Can you get a room by yourself?"

"Yes. Go." I nodded too vehemently, but those things happened when you played with vodka. I was ignoring it.

He nodded, and I leaned over to undo my seat belt.

"Jen?"

"Yeah?"

"Had you been sober, I would have kissed you."

"Had I been sober, I wouldn't have had the guts to ask the questions that got us there," I replied.

He smiled. "But I still have a date with you once you're sober, right?"

"No." I watched his face fall. "You need to make actual plans before I will admit that it's a date."

"Tomorrow? I will pick you up at your house at six?"

"Then it's a date."

CHAPTER 15

I walked into the resort pretending that I didn't feel like dancing. In my head I was Ginger Rogers, only in better heels, dancing with Fred Astaire. Outside I was calm and collected. Okay, there may have been a corny smile etched on my face, but I was mostly collected. All in all, I was pretty happy for a girl who'd lost her business partner, was shutting down her business, got kicked out of her house, and had just had an FBI agent drive off with her alcohol. I might not have been dancing, but I was close to it. I had a date. With a smoking hot FBI agent. Well, a smoking hot soon-to-be-ex-FBI agent. Maybe my life was turning around.

"Where did you hide it?"

Maybe not.

"Frank?" I turned around to see Frank hiding in the shadows of the lobby entrance, glaring at me.

"I know you have it, Jen. Where did you put it?"

"Put what?"

He reached over and grabbed my arm, pulling me into the empty stairwell. I felt like I had been pulled into a '90s movie. A stairwell? Who wanted to talk in a stairwell? Criminals and weird guys.

"Seriously, Jen. Where did you put it? Don't make me get serious."

"*Seriously*, I should make you get *serious*?" What kind of threat was that?

Hold up. *Threat*?

Was he *threatening* me? Frank? Short, pathetic, annoying, criminal Frank?

"*Shouldn't*. You *shouldn't* make me... it doesn't matter. Yes. We need the proof, Jen. Dad said he had proof. Told Donald that it would all come out if he came after us."

"Us?" Umm, I might really be in trouble. Like, real danger kind of trouble. And still drunk. Well, less drunk now that some adrenaline had kicked in. "Who is us? And what proof? I don't know what you're talking about."

Suddenly, he shoved me against the wall, my head hitting it with a crack that didn't sound good. My knees gave out and I would have dropped if Frank hadn't caught me.

What was happening?

I was fighting dizziness and alcohol, trying to wrap my brain around a situation that just couldn't make sense.

Lie. Could I lie?

About whatever *it* was?

"Sure. I have it." I knew he just told me more... "Proof. I have the proof."

Frank let go and turned away, too relieved to notice me slipping down the wall to the floor. Nor me reaching into my coat pocket. Where my phone was. I loved cell phones. And John. I loved John because he could keep his mouth shut in these situations. But I didn't have John's number.

Shit, my head hurt.

"She has it," Frank called up the stairwell.

Not working alone. Two against one poor, drunk girl. That wasn't fair.

"Good. Ask her where it is and let's get this over with."

"Where is it?" Frank dutifully asked.

Good to know Frank followed *someone's* directions. The few times I had given him any instructions, he had never followed.

I couldn't believe I was complaining about work. My head rolled back, and I tried to focus on Frank's face.

"You killed Henry." Wow. So not the point right now.

"No. We are screwed because of that asshole. Dan Ellson did it. We should have never let him in, but he found out and wanted a cut. He was tracking the trades."

"He was tracking your drinking habits, you idiot," the voice from above added.

"I didn't tell him. It didn't matter, he swore he wouldn't go after Dad. Stupid weakling. He knew that everything would come crashing down if he went after Dad." Frank hit the side of the wall with his hand to emphasize the point before turning back to me.

Okay. That seemed real.

"It would have been fine if your father had everything under control like he said he did. I knew we had a problem, but he insisted it was fine."

Oh my god. It had been them that Logan saw talking to Henry the night before. Not Dan. What did that mean for the murder?

"Maybe he had a plan and didn't get the time because of the murder," Frank argued back, his attention drifting towards the stairwell. Was there a chance I could sneak out while he wasn't looking—?

"Just get it!"

Nope.

"So, you need the… proof." Holding on to thoughts was harder than it should be. I struggled to stand, using the wall as support and moving slowly so I wouldn't upset Frank.

"Yes. Tell us where you put the proof Dad sent you and we'll let you go." He smiled, but I heard a snicker above me.

They weren't going to let me go. And I couldn't dial without looking at my phone. What stupid person thought up facial recognition as a lock? Because they should be here instead of me.

"House. The proof is at my house."

"Lies. We already searched your house."

Good point.

I needed to think. I was very smart. Like, exceptionally smart. Even drunk and concussed, I should've been able to outthink Frank and Donald. At least, I was pretty sure it was Donald up there.

Mail. I hadn't checked the mailbox.

"Mail. Your proof is in the mailbox."

"We checked your mailbox."

Well, weren't they thorough?

"Then it's coming tomorrow?"

Frank sighed and turned away from me, his hand going into his hair.

I took a risk and looked up, trying to see who the second voice belonged to, expecting to see Donald. Instead I saw a camera. Well, well. Donald hadn't known about Kenneth's new cameras. At least they would see what happened. And... maybe have a confession on film.

"Why? Why did you do it?" I asked Frank, my hand reaching back to feel the back of my head. No blood. Good.

"What? Take you? Or the insider trading?"

"Insider." My head really hurt, and I could feel the fuzzy feeling getting stronger. No. I couldn't lose consciousness yet.

"Tony had done it a few times, and Dad had missed it. But I caught it. Me. Then I demanded in. I wasn't as bad an accountant or CPA as you and Dad made me out to be."

Yes. Yes, he was, and this only proved it. Plus, he failed the test. One that we had nothing to do with. I didn't know why he was blaming us for his failing score.

"So, you helped him cover it up?"

"It was easy. The only one looking at their accounts was me. Dad was too busy and not as energetic as he used to be. Until the SEC contacted us, it was all too easy."

It's like he missed the point. Most crimes are easy. Until the cops show up.

"And did Henry know anything about it?"

"No. He was too busy. And trusted me. Unlike you."

Huh. I felt like that was missing a swear word. I definitely felt like there was supposed to be a b-word on the end of that sentence.

"And you think Dan killed Henry?" Confirmation is good.

"Had to be him. It wasn't Donald or me. We were fine until Dad ended up dead."

Yeah, I could see that he was really choked up about his dad.

"Henry covered for you!" I didn't hold back how mad I was about that.

"The worst that could happen was him losing his license. Dad was retiring anyway."

Neither was that true, nor the point. Crime. It was a crime. Was I the only one who had a problem with that?

"Get it over with," came the yell.

"You know, I can't believe I went on a date with you, Donald. I should have said no, but Dorothy just looked so expectant when she asked *for* you."

"Because I couldn't bring myself to ask out such an ugly bitch."

"Ooh. Breaking out the big words, huh?" Oh my god. What was I saying? Was this the panic? The vodka? Yes. I was blaming the vodka.

"Listen—" Donald came stomping down the stairs. Now both were on the tape. Idiots. "I could buy and sell you."

"No, your *family* can. You don't have any money, do you? Just a ceremonial position in the company that you couldn't keep."

"I can keep a job just fine."

"Like Operations Manager?"

"Yes. I will be. Grandmother knows I want it more."

"Oh, please. You don't even know where the security cameras are. You're too stupid to run a hotel."

I saw the fist.

I felt the contact.

I fell onto the ground with the force of the punch.

But none of that was as scary as the next sound I heard.

Click.

That was a gun. I was about to die. In this dingy stairwell. Over proof of a crime that was far less than the crime of murder they were about to commit.

On camera.

I was going to be killed by idiots.

There was something wrong with me, but even over the fear, I was angry. Angry that I had been brought down by two idiots who would make the stupid crimes hall of fame.

"You two are the dumbest morons on the face of this earth." My anger brought me to my feet, making me take a step away from the wall and toward them. "Are you kidding me? Do you even watch TV? When you decided to start your life of white-collar crime, did you even think to do a little freaking research into how to get away with it? This. This is why you will never be a CPA. Because not only are you an idiot, you can't see the obvious!" I was screaming at them by this point. I didn't even see the gun. Anger and vodka, making people make stupid mistakes since, well, I didn't know when vodka was invented, but it was a while ago.

"There are cameras everywhere, you two dipshits. You both confessed and threatened to kill me *on camera*. And what's worse? Murder. Murder is worse. You both are committing a huge crime to cover up a smaller one. I used to think people like you didn't exist. No one was that stupid. Now I owe Lark twenty bucks. Twenty. Because a freaking dressage trainer knows more about human nature than I do."

"Don't trainers spend all day working with people while you sit in your office working on a computer?" Frank asked, lowering the gun slightly in his confusion.

Did he…. he just corrected me. Nope. I refused. I refused to die at the hands of these two jokers. I was… going to find a way out. One-on-one I was pretty sure I could take them, but there were two of them. Then again, only Frank had the gun.

I was going to tackle him. That was all I had. Tackle. Flying tackle because, well, he still outweighed me by a lot. On three….

One. I could do this. I planted my feet, watching Frank who was still looking slightly confused about the whole situation.

Two. It was on. Bending knees. Donald rolled his eyes at Frank, who was the focus of his attention. Perfect.

Three. Go! I was flying.

"Put your hands up."

Shit.

It was true what they say: time slows down when you're about to die. My brain saw everything.

John coming in the staircase doors with his gun out.

Nic following close on his tail.

Frank's eyes going wide as he saw me coming.

Donald's eyes growing wide as he saw John and Nic.

Frank's finger on the trigger. Scratch that. *Tightening* on the trigger.

I was going to be shot.

This was going to hurt.

I squeezed my eyes closed as tight as I could, trying to throw myself aside by sheer force of mind. News flash—I had no telekinesis. No matter how much I mentally strained, I was still moving towards Frank and his gun.

Bang.

CHAPTER 16

Nothing hurt.

Could I be dead? Nothing hurt. Also, I should've landed on Frank by this point.

Wait, there were hands around my waist. Okay. Arms. There were arms around me. Was I just plucked out of the air? Was that even something someone could do? Wait. My ribs hurt. Make that tackled out of the air.

I peeked my eyes open.

Kenneth?

His blond hair was mussed, and we were both breathing hard. Like we had just run a race. One that had gotten us underneath the stairs. His back against the wall with me sprawled on top of him, his arms holding me tight, as we tried to process what just happened.

"Did you just tackle me before I was shot?"

"Yes." He pulled his arms away, putting me to the side, and we both leaned against the wall.

"That was kind of stupid."

He breathed harder. "Yes."

"Thank you."

"You're welcome." His head fell back against the wall.

"Jen? Kenneth? You guys okay?" Nic's body slowly came into view, his gaze and gun fixed on a target we couldn't see around the stairs.

"We're good," I told Nic before turning to Kenneth. "Actually, you hit the wall. Are you okay?"

"Fine." He still sounded a little winded.

"Did it knock the air out of you?" I asked, concerned that he might be hiding an injury. I knew people always said men did that, although I had never experienced it. My ex made a paper cut into a mortal death blow.

"No, just thinking through how stupid that was. I'll stop panicking in a moment," he admitted.

I laughed. I couldn't help it. I'd survived and Kenneth was funny.

"As much as I like hearing that sound, do you two think you can move to a safer location while we arrest these two? Once they're secure, we will come and talk with you, Jen." Nic took a second to throw me a concerned look before focusing back on the two idiots that got me here.

"Yeah, we will be in my office, if that works for you," Kenneth replied.

At Nic's nod, Kenneth rose, offering me a hand up before ushering me out of the stairwell too quickly for me to see more than Nic and John's backs.

A few seconds later, we were in a room that looked like it had been a guest room not so long ago. Two desks faced each other, and Kenneth dragged a chair out from the empty one for me to sit on before collapsing into the chair behind the bigger of the two.

"I can't believe that just happened," he sighed. "Donald. The gun. Jesus."

"I can't believe you tackled me to save me from a gunshot. That was crazy. Thank you."

He smiled shyly and blushed, reaching down to straighten things around his desk as a distraction. Once everything was perfect, he took a deep breath and looked me in the eye. "While you're feeling grateful, can we talk about a job?"

Ha. I knew that move. Hide your emotions in business. Wait....

"For me?"

He nodded.

Maybe I really was dead, and this was, well, not heaven. Kenneth was good-looking and everything, but I wanted better from heaven. Maybe this was reality?

More importantly, did I want to work for someone else? I would have financial security again, only this time someone else would have the burden of calling all the shots. It would limit my stress. But also my money. I could make more freelancing than working for a company.

Could I let go of control over my income? Accept that it would be regular and determined by hours and not my effort. Could I give up some of my security for happiness?

No. That wasn't right. Money hadn't done anything down in the stairwell. Friends did. Well, John and Nic did. And Kenneth.

"How did John and Nic get here so fast?"

"Dorothy saw Frank and called them. Something looked wrong and she was concerned. We were watching from the start."

Dorothy. Could I have been focusing on the wrong thing this whole time? Warmth flooded me. My friends. These people who I'd chosen to surround myself with had come through when I needed them. Maybe I had something more valuable than money.

Kenneth cleared his voice, clearly uncomfortable with the non-business topic. "It would be part-time, and out of this facility—"

"Yes." I cut him off. I didn't want to think about the details. Not right now. I was too numb with shock. "We can go over the details tomorrow." When I could remember them and focus. Plus, I was kind of feeling more impulsive tonight. Maybe Nic's attitude had inspired me.

"Excellent." He nodded as he stared down at his desk with a slight smile.

My eyes narrowed. He looked a little too happy with that.

"You took advantage of the situation." I was so impressed.

"Yes." There was no guilt on his face at all.

I was going to enjoy working for him. "Smart."

"I try." He took a deep breath. "That was really stupid." He turned the conversation back to his life-saving tackle.

"Yes. But I'm super glad you did it."

He nodded shooting me another shy smile.

"Did you guys get it all on camera?" I wanted to make sure at least I had done one thing right.

"Yes." His reply was short and clipped.

"Sorry about your brother." I knew what it was like to be betrayed by family. It wasn't fun.

"Sorry about your partner."

We sat in silence for a while.

"I need new shoes." Maybe some with bows. Or something in red.

"I have no idea what to say to that," he admitted.

"I don't think men are supposed to. If you did, you would either be the perfect man or gay." And I was pretty excited about my date with Nic, so I don't know that I could handle a perfect man right now. Or I would be, as soon as the shock wore off a little more.

"Well, then either my straightness is confirmed, or I need to work on perfection," he said, completely deadpan.

"I think we are going to get along fine."

He nodded, sending me a small grin. "Sorry Grandma set you up with Donald. He's a loser. She never thought you'd go."

"It's okay. Not the first time I've gone on a bad date. Plus, I'm more upset about how stupid he was when they tried to kill me."

"I know. We were watching. Nice speech by the way."

I glared. "You know, someone could have come in to save me."

"They had a gun."

I had nothing. It was a good point.

"Can I have a room for the night?"

"Want a suite?" He smiled with a mischievousness that I returned.

Sass. I could do sass. "Do I have to pay for it?"

"Can you forget being attacked by the owner's grandson the day after your partner was attacked and killed in the same hotel?"

"For a suite and a free massage, I can forget more than that." Oh my, a massage sounded good.

"Deal." He got out his phone and texted someone. "Eight a.m. work for you?"

"I take it back. You might be perfect," I admitted.

"If you didn't have a beau with a gun whom I'm trying to hire to run my security, I might have taken you up on that." He winked. It wasn't a smooth wink, like Nic's, all sexy and sin. No. His was more playful in a very stiff manner. He was too cute. Too bad I liked sexy. Maybe I wasn't meant for sweet. Maybe I was meant to be trading barbs with sexy.

"Business first. Where have you been my whole career?" I asked. I wouldn't have been stressed if I had known someone like him might be interested in hiring me here. I could make him a business legend.

"Learning to not be stupid on someone else's time." His expression never changed even though his eyes twinkled with humor.

"Jen?" Nic's head popped through the door and he looked around frantically before finding me. "You sure you're okay?"

His gaze was a little frantic, but it calmed down the longer he looked. I smiled at him. I was glad he wasn't leaving after this case was over. Wait... case. I frowned.

"They didn't do it."

"What?" He blinked several times, trying to process my comment.

Oops. Too rapid of a topic change.

"They didn't kill Henry. Dan did. Have you arrested Dan?"

His face went blank. "We'll talk about it tomorrow." His head popped back out.

"I don't think he is going to arrest Dan," I commented, my top teeth biting down on the side of my lip as I tried to figure out what I was missing.

I thought Dan did it.

Frank thought Dan did it.

Donald thought Dan did it.

How could we all be wrong?

"No, that face didn't look like it," Kenneth added, pulling himself up and straightening out his jacket. "Shall we go sign some paperwork? I would love to have you start work Monday."

"You really aren't going to give me time to process what just happened?" I was shocked. And impressed. There was something wrong with me, but I liked it. I was looking forward to work for the first time in years.

"Nope. You might change your mind. I would like to get you locked down before you start triple thinking it. Once you sign you will be all in." He smiled. Still no guilt. No shame. And he was willing to put his life at risk for another's. He was a good guy underneath it all.

Damn. Henry would have been drooling over getting his hands on a businessman like Kenneth. Maybe I should have gone after more of Watts Industries business before. *Henry, wherever you are, you were right.*

"You seem to think you know me pretty well."

"No, I just listen to my grandmother. She's a pretty smart lady."

Too true.

"I want vacation time."

"Two weeks." He offered.

Too easy. "Three."

"Two, with an increase to three in three years."

Since I had no idea what to do with the vacation, I guessed that worked. "I want Nic to have the same deal."

"I thought you guys weren't an item?"

"No. We're not."

He didn't look like he believed me. "Right then, sure, I can get Nic—" He glanced down as some paperwork before snorting. "—something similar."

My eyes narrowed. Did I care to find out what the snort was? No. No, I really didn't.

"Fine. Give me the details."

He did. The job title. What I would be doing. Not as interesting as some of my projects, but more interesting than others. The hours, which was only about twenty-four a week. It was all doable. And I knew Dorothy well enough to know they wouldn't have made the offer if it wasn't something she thought I would take. Plus, maybe I was in for a change. One that might need those two days off a week. I cut Kenneth off in the middle of a long description of the reporting structure. "I accept."

"Don't you want to know how much we will be paying you?"

"Please. I know my worth. You know my worth. We both know it. You will pay me what I deserve, or I walk. There will be no negotiation on that." I gave him a flat look, so he knew how serious I was about it.

He smiled at me. "You're right. We are going to get along just fine."

Kenneth handed me the pen. "Let's make this official."

CHAPTER 17

After a few minutes, there was a knock at the door. Kenneth opened it to reveal Nic, whose gaze went to me instantly and I flushed under his concern. Kenneth watched it silently, before nodding to us both and slipping out, closing the door behind him.

"Who killed Henry?" I demanded. Oops, wrong question. "Are you okay? No one was hurt?"

He smiled at my concern. "I'm fine. I wasn't the one tackling men with guns." His head tilted forward, hitting me with a glare communicating how unhappy he was with my choice of action as he put down some files on the desk.

"I was pissed. And not ready to let those two idiots kill me," I muttered, slightly embarrassed now that the adrenaline had dissipated.

"Yeah. I heard there is quite the speech for us to listen to later."

I blushed. "Henry?" I reminded him.

"You don't want to know about Frank and Donald?"

"No, I think I have a handle on Dumb and Dumber. I want to know why you aren't arresting Dan Ellson for Henry's death."

"Because Dan has an airtight alibi. He didn't do it."

"How airtight?"

"He would suffocate."

I was pretty sure that meant Dan was innocent. "How?"

"He was meeting with the DA at the time of the murder. The meeting was supposed to be at 11:30, but the DA was running early and so they rescheduled for 10. He didn't do it."

"Wait, the unsavory character he was meeting with before coming here were you guys?"

He glared at that but nodded to confirm. Well, that was kind of funny.

"So, he didn't do it. Frank didn't do it. Charlotte didn't do it. I didn't do it. Donald didn't do it. Who did? Because I'm out of people who knew who he was. Was it really just a robbery?"

"We have no clue." Nic collapsed into a chair, sending me a frustrated frown.

"Okay." What would help us? "More information."

"What?" He looked at me like I was crazy.

"I need more information. We have a problem. There must be a solution. We need more information."

"Well, you were there for most of the murder."

"Yep. Dude in all black ran me over."

"You sure it was a dude?" His eyes lit up.

"No." I was no help. "What about the wound?"

"You sure you want to know?"

No. "Yes."

"Point blank to the chest."

"Point blank?" Interesting. He had mentioned that before, but it hadn't registered. They would have had to walk up to Henry to shoot him. Why would Henry have just stood there? I mean, even I tried to leap at Frank. "And the room was searched, right?"

"Superficially, yes. Things were thrown around, but nothing taken."

"And the cameras?"

"The one in the hall outside his room was broken and had been for about a week, so we think that it might have been a coincidence. The other cameras didn't see anything."

"Nothing?" I had forgotten about that. How inconvenient.

"Nothing. We thought maybe they ducked into another room on the floor, but we went through the guest list and no one had any ties to Henry, Tony, or Dan."

Missing information. There had to be information missing. What would Henry tell me in this situation? *Start at the beginning.*

"Can I go home?"

"Why?"

"Well, other than the fact that I'm supposed to have evidence linking Donald to the crime? I want to check something."

"Sure." He picked up the files and his keys as he opened the door.

Wait. Those were my keys. He had my car? Oh my god. He had driven me here in my car and then drove off in it—

"Jen. Oh my god, you poor child." Dorothy was standing right outside, straightening up like she had been listening through the door.

"Kenneth told you?" I was disappointed. I thought he had more discretion than that.

"Nope." She held up her phone.

"You have got to be kidding me." Grabbing it out of her hands I started to read.

> *Perilous Accounts*
> *Just a little over an hour ago, our own Jennifer Ward was involved in an altercation with the man she was on a date with not three hours ago. Also involved was another man, believed to be her ex-business partner's son. What the altercation was about is unknown at this time, but witnesses in the resort lobby overheard shouts about 'proof'. We are assuming that this proof is in reference to the murder of Henry Boyd, who was killed in the same hotel, two days ago. Could Jennifer be involved in her business partner's death? Or could she be dating a criminal? We will follow up with the police when they make an announcement, as well as Miss Ward's*

response to accusations that she was
sleeping with a client.

"I'm not sure if I'm more insulted that she claimed I was sleeping with a client or that I was sleeping with Donald." That was insensitive. "Sorry, Dorothy. I'm sure that Donald has… good attributes that I have yet to see."

"I'm sure he does. When someone finds them, they will have to tell us," she said, shaking her head. "I can't believe he was involved. I think I'm more upset that he was that stupid."

"That's what got me, too," I admitted. "I can forgive being less than normal looking, but stupid? At that level? How is he from your genes?"

"If he didn't look so much like Kenneth, I would question that too."

Yeah, there really was no denying the two of them were related, even if one was a lot more attractive than the other.

"Kenneth is a good guy," I remarked.

She beamed, every inch a proud grandmother. "He is. He will make a fine leader for this company. Better than my husband was."

"Okay, then, I will just be heading home now."

"Hold on. I just wanted to tell you that Julia and Logan have decided to move here. In three weeks. Don't tell Lark. Or Brecken." She smiled broadly at me with a wink, obviously proud her plan had worked.

This was going to blow up in their faces. "Sure. Whatever. I know nothing. In fact, that sounds good. I

know nothing, saw nothing, you all did it without me."
I grabbed Nic's hand and started to pull him away.
"Remember, I'm a good little monkey statue."

"Got it. You two have fun." She smiled at the two
of us like she knew what we were up to, and it wasn't as
innocent as reality.

"We're not… He's not…" I dropped his hand.

"I'm just glad to see you welcoming our new
security expert so warmly." She waved, as she walked
away.

"She thinks we're sleeping together," I groaned.

"Is that a problem?" He asked with a smirk.

"Yes. Maybe. No… No, yes. Yes, it is a problem."

"Is that your final answer?"

"No," I groaned.

He paused, trying to figure out what question the
last no referred to. I used his distraction to get ahead and
walked to my car, which he obviously had been driving
around all night. Drunk me didn't even notice that when
he drove off earlier, he still had my car, but had noticed
the lack of alcohol. I didn't know if I liked what that said
about me. He paused to throw the file in the back seat
before getting into the driver's seat and starting the car.

"You remember how to get to my house?"

"Yes."

Good. I sat in silence, thinking. Henry had to have
guessed that I gave the feds the tip, so he started to
protect his son by faking records. But that didn't explain
why he took a vacation to my hometown. Or why he did
it with his family and the people involved in the case.

All the people involved. They were all here.

Donald, at Henry's request.

At the same time the FBI was knocking on my door to finalize the case.

The same time Dan was. Even worse, he was meeting with the DA. To make a deal. What did I want to bet that the deal included his partners?

Everyone was here. Dan was striking a deal.

What could he do with that?

He stayed in his dream suite.

Oh. MY. GOD.

Scarlett Johansson. I owed Lark an apology for making fun of her Marvel obsession.

"Do you have a list of all the people staying on that floor?" I asked.

"Yes."

"Can I see it?"

"Why not? Nothing else is going right on this case." He came to a stop outside the resort and reached behind me to grab his briefcase, flipping through it to find a folder before handing it to me. While I opened it, he moved back to the road and continued on. Part of me wondered why he had it on him, and in my car, but I was more focused on getting the information out of him before he realized he shouldn't be talking to a civilian.

I scanned the names. No... No... No.... Wait. I pulled out my phone, thankful for all those nights I stayed up watching reruns. Yep. Bless my nerdy little heart. Or the anxiety that made it hard for me to sleep.

"Maggie Hayward."

"We didn't talk to her, but she is a waitress from San Francisco. She was just here for the weekend. Checked out about thirty minutes before the murder. No connection to Henry."

"I wonder what car she drives." Could she have been in the car speeding out of the driveway?

"Why? We couldn't find a link."

"That's because she's connected to Natasha Romanova, or Natalia Romanova depending on your expertise, most recently played by *Scarlett Johansson*." And knowing that meant I needed to stop letting Lark control our movies.

"How?"

"Maggie Hayward is the name of the girl who becomes Nikita."

"The assassin?" Nic's face was still blank.

"And Scarlett Johansson was recently Natasha Romanova. Otherwise known as Black Widow."

"An assassin. I'm seeing a trend."

"Yep." I was gloating. I tried to hold it in, but it was a full-out gloat.

"So, you think someone hired an assassin? To kill an accountant who already confessed to everything?"

"Nope. You're forgetting something. The emails to Scarlett Johansson were *from* Henry."

Nic pulled off onto the side of the road again.

I glanced over at Nic's distracted expression. I was pretty sure he was thinking about the case. Not making out in a car. Because that would be very immature, but I had to admit that after all these missed chances, I was starting to get curious. I mean, lots of people say it's sexy. Maybe it was time to see for myself.

"You think he killed himself," Nic breathed out the words, obviously following my thoughts.

Talk about a topic change. I couldn't believe I let myself get so distracted. "Yep."

"That explains the gun," he muttered.

"The gun?" There was a gun found, and no one told me? I was pissed. And a civilian. They didn't owe me an explanation. How inconvenient.

"Dan came back to his room to find the murder weapon. Only he had a federal agent with him."

"Henry set him up." Genius. Also, wow. He must have really disliked Dan. More than Tony.

"Yes." Nic's eyes were unfocused and moving rapidly. Whatever he was thinking, he was thinking it hard.

"Why would he go to such lengths?"

"Dan was going to turn over his accomplices. That was what the meeting was about," Nic admitted. "He signed a document incriminating Frank at the meeting and was going to sign one about another partner, who we know assume is Donald, later that day. Before the murder."

Haha. I was right. I was a criminal crime-solving genius. And so humble.

"You think that he committed suicide to incriminate Dan? Dan goes down for Henry's murder and it discredits Dan's plea deal that blamed Frank for the fraud?"

"I guess. I mean, it might have worked had the timing been better. Everyone has readily believed it was Dan, even without any evidence."

"I still think that it was stupid," I grumbled.

"It is elaborate," Nic agreed. "You really think he sent you evidence?"

"No." I sighed. "He probably lied to make sure that they didn't do anything stupid." That also meant that he had set me up to find his body. Why? Why would he want me to do that?

"Why are you looking so sad?" Nic asked.

"Henry set me up to find him." And that hurt.

"You were supposed to meet at nine, remember? I bet he moved the assassination to accommodate and the timeline got messed up," Nic admitted. "Henry was told about our second search ahead of time. Well, to be honest, I'm guessing he overheard the conversation during one of our last interviews."

"You sure your boss isn't trying to get rid of you?" I glared. "Talking about the investigation in front of one of the perpetrators seems stupid."

"One, you are using the word 'stupid' a lot tonight. Two, I was talking to her, so no, she isn't trying to get rid of me."

He glared, but I just shrugged. They made the mistake. I just pointed it out.

"Why didn't you have a warrant ready?" It occurred to me that if this had been planned, they should have.

"Honestly? We were going to, but it got held up at the last minute. I went to your house to see if we could get in anyway, but you were stubborn." He gave me a sheepish smile. "I was on my way to your house to serve the warrant when I ran into you at the resort on the morning he was killed. I was delayed by another case." He sat for a second. "That's a lie."

Okay. I just waited for him to continue.

"I came a day early to see if I could fix my original impression."

Wow. "You failed."

"Yeah. It didn't go the way I wanted. I panicked a little."

That was so cute. But we were talking about Henry.

"Then who was supposed to find Henry?"

"Probably Carrie. She had a meeting at ten-thirty."

That made me feel better. We pulled up at my house. I studied it without leaving the car. I didn't know what to do. My reasons for coming here were voided. If we weren't looking for evidence, what were we looking for?

"Why aren't you getting out?" Nic asked, after a second.

"I don't know what I'm looking for." I sighed. "The house has been searched twice by the FBI. Once by Dumb *or* Dumber. One of the two. I haven't chosen which Frank is. Dumb or Dumber. All the ideas I had were about Henry's murder. Not suicide. There probably isn't even a letter with proof, which explains why no one can find it." I pursed my lips, studying the house again, as if something might occur to me. I mean, that should be what happened, right? I would have an epiphany and know right where it is. That happened in TV shows.

Maybe I needed someone to say something inspiring? Where are all the nosy gossip queens when I need them?

"Do you want to go back to the resort?" Nic asked, putting his hand on my thigh to reassure me.

Well, that wasn't helping me think.

"No. Maybe we can look around and see if anything inspires me?" There had to be something. Maybe if I went in and thought about it.

"Sure. Worth a try." Nic shut the car off and opened his door, following me up the walkway.

I took the keys and unlocked the front door, looking around to see if anything looked disturbed or a good place to hide something that may or may not be evidence. I flicked on my lights and glanced around.

Chaos. Complete chaos.

Nothing was where it was supposed to be.

Books were thrown across the floor. My throw pillows were on the ground, making walking hazards. My drawers were all open, their contents strewn about the floor.

I was going to be sick.

"It's going to take me forever to get everything back in its place." I spun around, trying to take it all in. Or avoid taking it all in. I couldn't tell. Or decide.

I needed air. More air. Different air.

I needed to start now.

I couldn't leave it like this.

Everything needed to be put away.

Now. Everything in its place.

Nic grabbed my hand and brought it in front of him, forcing me to turn into him. "It can wait. I can help you. But do it tomorrow. After your massage."

No. I couldn't relax until I started cleaning—

His eyes had me caught and I could feel the pressure in my chest relaxing. "It can wait," he repeated, brushing my cheek with his hand.

I breathed out. "You're right." It could wait.

"Of course, I am." He smirked before his face went serious. His eyes hooded and dropped to my lips. "How drunk are you still?" His voice had dropped an octave. And gotten rumbly.

I liked that. I stepped closer, smiling shyly at him. My chest was still heaving for breath, although for a completely different reason. His hand clenched on mine and pulled slowly, encouraging me closer. I leaned into him, lifting up on my toes to get as close as I could to his lips. He—

"Please don't."

I screamed and pushed Nic away.

There was someone else here. A female someone else.

Screaming and pushing him away ended up being stupid, since he had been leaning toward me when I pushed, which meant he wasn't balanced. He took a step backward, but his foot met a throw pillow, tripping him and causing him to land on his butt, his phone sliding across the floor with a clang.

"Okay, I take it back. That was funny. Feel free to throw the FBI agent around more." The female voice was definitely amused.

I didn't recognize the voice, even after my panic settled a little and I spun around, searching for the source. Only the movement itself told me that someone was in the shadows. She was dressed in all black, covering even her face and hair. I wouldn't be able to tell the police anything about her.

Typical. Once again, I was useless.

"Don't even think of reaching for the gun, FBI." More movement, but this time I recognized enough to know what it was. A gun. Another gun.

What was up with tonight? And I need to work on my stress responses. The screaming thing might have just gotten us killed. I was a *CPA*. I could handle stressed out CEOs and angry managers. I didn't scream when startled. Except for tonight. Then again, CEOs didn't jump out of the dark at me.

I glanced over at Nic, who had been reaching for his gun. His hand stopped and moved up so that she could see he wasn't reaching for it.

"What do you want?" My voice sounded reasonably calm for someone who just screamed and shoved my only protection to the floor.

"I was here trying to complete my promise, but this whole thing has been a FUBAR from start to finish." The disgust was clear in her voice.

"Sorry." Wait? Did I just apologize to an assassin? I was pretty sure that was taking manners too far.

She made a sound that I'm pretty sure was a muffled laugh. "That's okay. Well, here's your letter. Sorry I couldn't give you the clandestine spy experience. It was supposed to appear out of nowhere, leaving you to wonder how. Nothing has gone the way it was supposed to. This town is… something else."

"The town?" Hmm, was it a character flaw that I couldn't keep my mouth shut when faced with a gun? Because it seemed like a character flaw. One Lark shared. We were born to be best friends.

"Do you know that the owner of the hotel personally checked in on Henry? Three times, right around the time of your meeting." She threw an envelope at my feet. "I had to keep hiding in the bathroom because your meeting made our timeline so close. I had to get the job done before his meeting with the Fed." The hand not holding the gun started emphasizing her words. Evidently, she was a hand talker. "I do not hide in bathrooms. Not for anything. Even money. Then brunch ended early. And you were late. Then you had a Fed with you." She shook her head. "FUBAR."

I had no words. I don't even want to know what I looked like as I tried to piece together that information. I just kept blinking like it was out of focus.

"And before that was that stupid reporter and the cake. Who cares about some stupid boob cake? But no, she followed me all the way to the resort, dogging my steps because I *might* have witnessed the fiasco while thinking about buying a doughnut. I wasn't even there, but she saw someone outside, and decided to follow me. Because I *might* have seen something. I was trying to get a doughnut because Henry had said they were so good. That you had told him you loved them. And who sells nuts in a bakery, anyway?"

"They got married." For the love of... I was pretty sure that question was rhetorical. Why did I answer it? Also, he told her to try the doughnut because I liked them. I was going to cry.

"They got married? I guess that makes sense. A boob cake for a bachelor party." She had been the witness.

I shrugged. "The bakery and nut shop. It *was* two shops. Then the owners got married. Destroyed the wall on their wedding day."

The gun sank slightly as she thought about it. I thought. I mean, I couldn't really see much behind the mask. "That is ridiculously romantic."

"Isn't it? They have a photo behind the counter." I sighed, because, well, even death didn't stop it from being the most romantic story I had heard of in real life. Two people and businesses becoming one.

"Is this really going on?" Nic asked, drawing both of our attentions. He sat on the floor, his abs holding him up as his hands were still in the air. Rock hard abs. He wasn't even struggling.

I bit my lip to not say anything snarky. Or overtly sexual.

"He's been holding that position for a while. He must have some nice abs." The assassin ran her eyes over him appreciatively. Or what I guessed was appreciatively because, well, mask.

"He does," I confirmed, because maybe she wouldn't kill us if she thought he was hot. A girl could hope.

"Nice catch. He looks like a keeper. At least when there aren't things behind him to trip on." She started moving toward the back door. "Well, it's been fun, but I'm done with this town and this assignment from hell. Enjoy your letter."

"Wait!" I couldn't believe that I was going to ask this, but I had to know. "Why did Henry not just shoot himself?"

She stopped and studied me. "You didn't figure that out? It's pretty easy to tell when someone kills themselves. Cops can find that evidence pretty quickly." She looked at Nic, then shrugged. "And it's hard to plant evidence if you're dead. I killed both birds with one stone. Or bullet, in this case."

"He did it. For sure. He killed himself." I knew that. Why did hearing her say it hurt more than when I first guessed?

"I'm sorry. Read the letter. Maybe he explained it." Then she was gone, melting into the dark like a shadow. Nic jumped up to follow her but came back a few minutes later without an assassin and frowning.

"She's a ninja," I breathed.

"She broke your backlight. She is not a ninja," Nic muttered, giving me an unamused glare. "I can't believe you were bonding with an admitted assassin."

"What? That story is romantic." Don't say it... don't say it... "And she didn't admit to being an assassin. She only said clandestine spy. That could mean anything."

I didn't know his scowl could get worse. Maybe it was more of a glower? Glare? It was too angry for a frown. Maybe scowl was the right word.

"I got downed by a couch pillow." He was scowling even harder. "Why do you even have couch pillows? Who needs them? Everyone just jostles until they are out of their way. They aren't even used."

"They're throw pillows," I corrected. "And they're pretty." Not the point....

"We could have died. Because of couch pillows."

He was kind of right. About the dying, at least. I decided it wasn't worth trying to correct him on not calling them throw pillows.

"She thinks you're sexy." Distracting him with his own ego.

He still had his eyes narrowed, but his mouth started to creep up. "And a catch," he added.

"Mmm, I don't know." I pretended to think about it. "I do admit sitting there for the whole conversation holding yourself up by your abs alone was sexy." Not as sexy as his eyebrow thing, but I wasn't about to tell him that.

He smiled at me, his eyes burning hot. I didn't think he was thinking about the assassin anymore. I blushed but kept eye contact. I could do this.

He started walking towards me slowly, prowling with a heat that I could feel even before he touched me.

"Normally, I would go slow. Let you savor each moment, each contact." His arms went around me and pulled me flush against his body. "But the girl in black was right. This town is hell on plans, and I have no intention of letting this moment go again."

He kissed me.

Stars. I was pretty sure I was seeing stars. I grabbed him tighter and pulled until there was no space between us, chest to chest, hips to... well, I was going to call it his little gun for the moment. It would give him more temptation to let me see it. At some point his hand had fisted in my hair, yanking my head into the perfect position for his kiss.

"Stand on the box..."

Nic's phone started blaring out a country song and we both broke away. He jumped over the couch cushion that was sitting in the center of the room to get to it where it had fallen during his landing. I collapsed into a heap on the couch, since my knees were still somewhere stuck in the mind-blowing kiss we just had.

"Was that *Something Bad*?" I couldn't stop staring at Nic. I didn't see a country music fan. Cool.

"Nic." He answered the phone giving me a glare over the couch. "Yeah, Carrie. We made it." He listened for a few seconds taking a seat on the other couch. "We found something, but we haven't opened it yet. Meet you back at the resort?" He nodded absently as he listened before hanging up.

"Country music?"

"It was Carrie. My boss."

"She picked it, or you made it her ringtone because they're both Carrie's?"

"Umm, both?" He looked a little guilty.

I thought about what I knew about him... and what I knew about Carrie Underwood songs. "You were using *All-American Girl*, weren't you? And she made you change it?"

He scowled. "You're lucky that kiss was amazing, or I would be rethinking this."

I snorted. "No, you wouldn't." I climbed over the obstacles to get to him, smiling my most seductive smile.

"We need to go back to the resort," He groaned as he watched me coming.

I was pretty sure I nailed seductive based on the way his eyes watched every movement I made.

"We will." I slipped into his lap. "After I remind you what putting up with my sass gets you."

I'd changed my mind about the perks of bad boys.

CHAPTER 18

A few minutes later, we were back in my car driving to the resort with the envelope in hand. Well, Nic's right hand. His right was wrapped around my left as he drove, rubbing soft, soothing circles on the back of my hand.

Carrie met us in the parking lot, looking slightly annoyed.

"Where have the two of you been?" She demanded as we got out of the car.

Nic smiled, his eyes heating as he looked over at me.

I blushed and distracted her by pointing to Nic's hand. "Envelope."

She came over and grabbed it. "What's in it?" She looked at both of us confused when she saw that it was still sealed.

I shrugged. I had debated knowing. Debated opening it and finding out what Henry's last message was to me. But I already had a pretty good idea of what he did, and even though I got that he did it for the love of his child, I couldn't take any more tonight. I wanted to let the Feds deal with it. I was going to go get some sleep. Unfortunately alone, because leaving the Feds to

251

deal with it meant Nic was going to have to stay there too. A yawn forced its way out. Maybe that wasn't so unfortunate.

"I don't care." And with that I walked past them, swinging an overnight bag over my shoulder as I went through the doors and to the desk where I was hoping someone would have a room key, as promised. It was freeing. Not caring. I had my answer. I was free. I had a new life, a new job, a new man… life was good. For the first time in years I didn't listen for my heels, for the soothing tap. I didn't need to.

"I'll talk with you tomorrow," Nic yelled from behind me.

I waved acceptance. "After nine. I have a massage." I looked at the front desk girl, who had to be maybe eighteen, but I didn't recognize her. "Do you have a key for Jennifer Ward?"

She searched the desk without smiling and gave me a key with my name attached to it with a sticky note.

"Here you go. If you go up the elevators to the fourth floor, it will be on your right."

"Got it. Thanks."

One elevator ride later I was in the room, which surprisingly looked very little like the room Henry had been murdered—I mean, the room Henry had been shot in. Since we were questioning if it was murder or not.

I was having serious doubts. The plan was very elaborate, having multiple moving pieces, several of which went wrong. Why would he hire an assassin when he could have just… Okay, I admitted, I couldn't think of another way to discredit Dan. On the other hand, I was pretty sure that if Frank was my son, I would have let him hang.

Even the assassin had said everything went wrong. Definitely the sign of a plan that had too many moving parts. And maybe we were doing Henry a disservice assuming that he was the one in contact with the assassin. Maybe it was Frank in Henry's email. But then why would he deny it later? Plus, his father was covering for him. Why kill him?

It wasn't a good night's sleep. On the other hand, the massage was wonderful, and by nine the next morning, I was feeling like a new person. One that had a new job that didn't have a pending criminal charge looming over it. A new boss, who I was pretty sure I would get along with just fine. Lots of hours to do... stuff. Hmm, I would need to start thinking about a new hobby or two soon. When the text came in from Nic asking me to meet him in Kenneth's office, I was no longer stressed. I was ready to put this behind me. Well, the case behind me.

Nic was another story.

I knocked on the door and Carrie let me in with a smile.

"Jen. It's so nice to see you again."

"Carrie," I greeted. I didn't know why she was so excited and, frankly, it made me a little suspicious. "How's everything going?"

"Great. Great. Please sit down."

Yep. Those are never good words. Those words are what people hear when they're about to be let go. Or get upsetting news.

I sat in the same chair I used last night, and Carrie took Kenneth's.

"So, the envelope you got last night did have evidence to link Donald as the source of the information on the companies, information he got by leveraging his family's contacts and listening at meetings he wasn't supposed to be at." She waited to see if I had any questions.

I didn't. Should I? I thought about it. Nope. Not a one.

"There was no mention of Frank, but since they attacked you we knew they both were in on it," she continued. "We also talked with Charlotte this morning. She broke and told us that it was all a set-up. Henry was dying of pancreatic cancer and only had a few months to live, anyway. He figured this was an easier and a better option than letting the cancer take him. He had approached her after he learned about the cover-up and his cancer and they came up with this plan. She did it to help try and save Frank, too. I'm sorry for your loss."

I nodded. It hurt, but I was angry. And maybe a few other emotions, too. I would have to process it later. After everyone was gone, and I was alone.

She shifted her weight, her gaze flitting away from me for a second before meeting my eyes again. "There was also an apology. Do you want to read it now? The letter is going into evidence. This might be the last time for a while."

I looked at the paper taunting me from inside the sealed evidence bag. Did I want to know what he said? No. I might regret it later, but no. I didn't want to know. I wanted to let it go. "No. I'm good. I don't want to read it."

"Nic told us of your run-in with the girl last night. Can you remember any more details?"

"More than a trained professional like Nic? No. She was female. She was funny. She used military terms. She's a ninja. Other than that, I have nothing. Not even a height or nationality. There was no accent. But that could be trained." I was reaching, trying to be helpful and failing.

She nodded, as if that was what she expected. "Well then, the cases are being closed. We will be gone by the end of the day."

"Nic?" Oops. That was too telling.

Her smile took on a gloating lift at the question. "He's staying. He's taking vacation until his last day and then he will start his job here."

Well, then.

"Thank you." I didn't really know what more to say, so I just stood to shake her hand before she slipped out the door, leaving me standing in Kenneth's office, not knowing where to go. I guess it was time to check out. I opened the door, trying to figure out what I should do first. Cake? Or cleaning?

"I have a promise to fulfill today and I'm hoping you could help me." Nic's voice came from my left, and I jumped when I looked to see him waiting by the door.

I didn't scream though, so I was willing to take it as progress.

"A promise?" I echoed, a little confused. And distracted by his lips.

"Yeah, I promised a beautiful girl I would help her clean her house. Do you think you might be able to help me keep it?" He had caught on to my fascination and his smile turned wicked.

"Is that you asking to come home with me?" I can't believe I just said it that way, but okay... okay, I could roll with it.

"Umm, well, I mean, yes, but not in the way it sounded." He blushed.

I just did my best eyebrow lift. "You sure?" I looked him up and down. "I would have thought you would keep a more open mind."

"Open for anything," he said with a smirk. Before wincing.

"Yeah, that was bad." I shook my head.

"But you like me, anyway."

"Are you staying in Barrow Bay?" I licked my lips, suddenly extra nervous even though I knew the answer already. "You know, for good?"

"Forever," he whispered, his hand cupping my cheek and raising it up so that my eyes met his.

"Those are some big words," I whispered.

"It's only one word," He corrected. "And I like challenges."

Fireworks. His kiss was like fireworks.

I should have ruined my life earlier.

Thank you for reading Number's Up, book one of the Barrow Bay Mysteries.

Lark and the Barrow Bay crew will be returning with the next installment coming in Fall 2019.

Check out https://annabellehunter.com/newsletter/ to receive updates about upcoming releases.

Want to know how it started?
Check out this free excerpt from Leg Up, book one of
the Lark Davis Mysteries:

CHAPTER 1 - LEG UP

There was a severed leg on my porch.

I would like to say I checked to confirm it was real, or gasped in horror, or called the police, or heck, even screamed. But nope. I stood there, my chin almost hitting my chest as I looked down at the leg in front of me. Thank goodness Hailey was with her father this week, so they could spend some time together before school was back in session at the end of the month. Good parents didn't let their children see dead body parts. Plus, I didn't have the money for that much therapy.

I wouldn't be here if I'd cleaned out my garage like I promised myself I would. If I had, I could've made it to my truck and driven away without even glancing at my front door. Could this be karma for not unpacking all my boxes? No, that was just silly. I was pretty sure karma for a messy garage wasn't a dead body part.

Thoughts like these were probably the reason I was going to hell.

Checking my watch, I pushed some of my light brown hair out of my face and confirmed I would be late to teach my first riding lesson of the day. This was not the way to start my Tuesday. I looked back down. I was probably going to be late for a lot more than that. Sighing, I texted my morning clients and my working student to let them know I would try to arrive by noon.

I looked at the leg again. Could it be fake? I mean, who gets a limb on their doorstep without the corresponding body? Inching forward and holding my breath, I looked closer. Yep. Definitely real. It already smelled enough that I didn't need to breathe for the stench to hit me.

Hmm. I wondered how long it would take for the cops to get here? I heard about how slow the response time was, but I would think a body part would rank high enough to get them here sooner than… I looked at my phone and swore. *Shiitake mushrooms.*

Dialing 911, I waited through the hold message until a female voice came on the line.

"Nine-one-one, what's your emergency?"

"Severed leg."

"Excuse me?"

"I found a severed leg."

"Is it still bleeding? Do you hear noises coming from nearby that might indicate where the owner of the leg is?"

I looked down. I hadn't moved since opening the door, instead my training kicked in, keeping me frozen as I processed. After years of working with horses, it was amazing how quickly I learned to stay calm and still, especially when facing an animal who was depending on me to tell it what to do. And panic was never the right answer. Yeah, I had learned to stay outwardly serene during a crisis. But I had yet to learn how to stop myself from being sarcastic when panicked. I really needed to, though.

"Nope. It's stopped bleeding, and there's no puddle of blood underneath it, so I would guess the previous owner is not around."

"Previous owner?"

"The dead guy."

"Do you know he is dead?"

"Well, there's a leg sitting on my front porch, so unless a hospital around here had a thigh amputation and got remarkably careless with the body part, I would guess the person it came from is dead."

"Ma'am, we ask that you give us the facts and not any assumptions." Well, that came off irritated.

"Okay. I opened my door and there was a severed leg on my porch."

"And you are sure it is human?"

"Yes. I'm sure."

"May I ask how?"

"Well, the shoe was a good indication, but the tattoo really clinched it for me."

"Again, ma'am, we ask for just the facts."

The operator was telling me to hold the sarcasm. Probably a good call. If only I could.

"When can the cops get here?"

"We have a unit en route now."

"Thank you. Can I hang up now? I have things to reschedule. And a garage to clean."

"A garage?"

"It doesn't matter. Can I go?"

"No. I need your name and your address."

"Larklyn Davis." I rattled off my address. "Wait. If I just gave you my address how did you have a unit en route?"

"Are you sure you're not in any danger?" She asked.

"Other than from my homeowner's association fining me for this, yes. I'm safe," I muttered.

Today. The garage would get cleaned today.

"Has the homeowner's association made threats in the past towards your safety?"

"What? No! They'll just… you know what? I'm hanging up now. Thank you for sending the cops." I hung up before she could ask me any more questions I would probably answer sarcastically. I ducked back inside the house and pulled a chair out to sit down, keeping an eye on the leg just in case. From inside my house, even with the door open, the smell wasn't too horrible, so I guessed whoever the leg belonged to hadn't been dead long. My phone rang, and I looked down at it. Missy, my working student, was calling. I gave her lessons in trade for doing all the jobs I didn't want to do. In other words, I couldn't live without her.

"Hey, Missy."

"You texted you'll be late. You never miss lessons. What happened?" Her voice was concerned, and I sighed. She was right, I couldn't afford to miss any paid lessons.

"Severed leg."

"Damn. Did the vet ask you to hold another horse from next door again?"

My next-door neighbors at the stable, while nice people, were awful animal owners. No matter how many times I explained to them what kind of fence to use for horses versus other animals, they insisted on using regular chain link. Since they used the same vet as me, it inevitably ended up with them coming to the barn, wringing their hands and pleading for me to come help. And, the sucker for a horse in distress that I am, I always do.

"Not this time. Human leg."

"You found a human leg?"

"To be more accurate, someone delivered a human leg to my front door."

"I didn't know Amazon got into the body parts business." Horse people. We had a morbid sense of humor.

"Thank goodness they don't. Imagine if it had been in a box? I would have just brought it in, gone to work, and it would have taken days to get rid of the smell."

"We're going to hell, aren't we?" Missy stated.

"I debated driving off before calling the cops. This conversation is just the cherry on top."

"So, you're waiting for the cops now?"

"Yep. Something tells me this'll take a while."

"I guess that something is the leg."

"Har har. I'm hanging up now."

"Wait! Schedule?" Missy threw out before I could press the end button. Son of a gun. How was I going to do this?

"Can you take Jill and Katie's lessons this morning and we'll split the fee? Also, let's lunge Donner and Joey. I'll just ride them Sunday to make up for today's ride." So much for my promise to myself for two whole days off this week. I scheduled my work week so that I got Mondays off and, if I got everyone ridden and there was no show, the occasional Sunday. Before this morning, this week had been looking like one of my few short ones. "Hopefully this won't take long, and I'll be there in time to ride everyone else and do my evening lessons."

"Got it. Good luck. Let me know if more body parts show up."

"Go away." I hung up and checked the time again. Five minutes had passed and still no cops. I eyed the leg again. It looked like a man's leg based on the amount of curly brown hair. Creating a thick layer, the hair covered most of the leg, obscuring a tattoo on the back of the calf. The tattoo looked like an eagle perched on a globe. Wasn't that a military thing? I thought for a second before I took out my phone and confirmed. Marines. The leg belonged to a Marine. Or used to. Maybe still? Did bodies keep possession of their parts once dead? I went to google that answer but I stopped myself. Those kinds of searches never looked good. Nothing else about the leg stood out, and I was left without any other clues to whose it was.

My phone beeped, and I looked down to see that the local blog for town news had alerted me to a news article. I read the first line: *Need a Leg up? Larklyn Davis has you covered.*

Son of a donkey's uncle. I opened it up and read.

> *At 7:08 AM Tuesday morning, Larklyn Davis called the state 911 line to report finding a leg on her property. It is believed, at this time, she found it while cleaning in her garage, which we all know she needs to do if she ever wants to catch a man again. She also complained of threats from the homeowner's association. We will follow up with more information as soon as it becomes available.*

Shiitake mushrooms! My head dropped into my hands. How did Lindsey get all this information? She had to be sitting close to the dispatch to hear the phone call come in. Being a blogger in a town of 1,000 people couldn't be *that* boring. Alright, maybe it was, but she published the article before the cops even arrived. Where *was* Benny? I dialed the direct line for the station and waited.

"Barrow Bay Police Station. Gladys here. How can I help you?"

"Hey, Gladys. It's Lark. Any chance anyone will swing by my house and pick up this leg anytime soon?"

"Lark! Heard you were having a hard morning, hon. How are you doing?"

Deep breaths, I told myself. Just keep taking deep breaths.

"Fine, Gladys. Fine. About the leg?"

"Oh yes. The boys were just listening to your 911 call. Best laugh we've had all day."

Snickerdoodles.

"I don't suppose Lindsey was there when you were listening to it?" The Barrow Bay Police Department was mostly one big room with no walls. Just desks. This led to lots of jokes and camaraderie. It also led to everyone hearing everything. There were no secrets in the police department. It also didn't help that the dispatch was in the center of the room.

"How did you know? Such a sweet girl. I think she has a thing for one of the boys."

No, she had a thing for being the first person to know anything, and then telling everyone as quickly as humanly possible.

"Just a guess. Leg?"

"Oh yes. Chief Jenkins will be on his way."

Good. The police station was only around the corner, so Benny should be here—

"Wait, *will* be on his way?"

"Yes, dear. He needs to finish his coffee first."

Why did I move out of the city again? Oh yes. I wanted to be anywhere my ex-husband wasn't. And personal small-town charm sounded lovely while I was visiting Gran after my mom and dad died. I was currently re-evaluating that decision.

"I don't suppose if I offer him a fresh cup with my special gourmet blend, I might convince him to come out right away?"

"Well, aren't you just a doll? I'm sure that would do the trick." Gladys had embraced the small-town cliché a little too hard, and I had given up trying to get her to stop using pet names within months of moving here. Some things would never change.

"Well then. I'm brewing it for him right now. Will he be here in a few minutes if I throw in a danish?" I didn't need breakfast, but I needed to get back to work.

"I'm sure that would work, dear. You have a better day!" With that, Gladys hung up the phone to go tell Benny about my bribe.

When I moved here with Hailey last year, a year after my divorce and months after the deaths of my parents, I knew trying to have a stable in a town so small would be hard. At the time, simplifying my life and only having what I needed sounded good. Rebellious. Freeing. What utter bull-puckey. The only thing I escaped was having extra spending money.

That wasn't entirely accurate. I was what they termed 'independently wealthy' thanks to my inheritance from my parents. It was how I bought the stable just out of town and my house close to the main street. All I got out of the divorce was custody of Hailey during the week, most weekends as our schedules would allow, and my three horses. The first was my current top mount, and I hoped to show him within the coming year at Prix St. George in the San Francisco dressage show circuit. The second was my old show master, who I used to do lessons. The third was my baby, a four-year-old warmblood mare I nicknamed Twice. As in 'don't make me say it twice.' Or, if no one was around, Shrew.

Twice was really my daughter's horse, and she had hit a 'My Little Pony' stage when it came time to name the barn's newest addition those years ago. Pleading eyes and a happy smile later, my next great mount was named L.D. Twilight Sparkle. I refused to use Twilight or Twily as her barn name, because I was not going to associate her with the show any more than necessary. Princess of Friendship, she was not. If the stupid mare didn't worship the ground my daughter walked on, she would have been sold in the divorce. Or I would have taken her mother instead. But no. The little mare fought every command but loved Hailey like they were born to be together. And she hated everyone else. She put up with me most days, but we'd argued over who was in charge too many times for me to list her as my favorite.

I had eight other horses in the barn: four in boarding, and four in some sort of training. Just enough to cover my bills for the feed and shavings, but I was hesitant to get in the habit of dipping into my savings. I still hoped that I could make my business work.

Chief Jenkins, or Benny as we all called him, pulled up right about then, and I had coffee and a pastry waiting for him. Coffee was my one indulgence, and I spent the extra money to have my favorite brand shipped to me, even now that I lived in the middle of nowhere. Chief Jenkins also shared my love of all things caffeinated, a habit he says he picked up in the Marines, and his eyes lit up at the sight of the to-go cup in my hand.

"Lark! Always a pleasure to see you!" His large frame moved slowly up the sidewalk. He was older, somewhere in his early 60s, but my favorite of his features were his eyes. There was something about them that pulled you in. They always seemed to be smiling at you, no matter what was happening, as if his good nature just couldn't be contained.

"You too, Chief. I expect you're going to want to take in the leg before your coffee?" I pointed at the offending limb before pulling the coffee back away from him. I had been around long enough to know that this was a negotiation. We didn't do anything the same in this town.

"Ahh honey, you know I can't touch it until the coroner comes and looks."

No. No, I hadn't known that. My shoulders dropped.

"How long?" I asked as I surrendered the cup and my negotiating position.

He took the coffee after carefully placing a sheet over the limb and stepping over it to come in the house.

"About three hours. Dr. Stevenson is on vacation, so we have to call the county coroner."

"I don't suppose I can leave while you handle this? I mean, it's a leg. That is the extent of my knowledge. I could just give you a key to lock up and—"

"No can do. Need to ask you some questions. Investigate and all that. Detective Hernandez is on his way." He watched as I slumped, resigned that I wasn't going anywhere.

"Can't you do the interview?" I pleaded. "I mean, it isn't like I know anything. Do we really have to wait for Hernandez?"

"And step on the toes of my favorite detective after I worked so hard to get him? Nope." He patted my shoulder. "Should have left for work after the call, honey. Would have been able to get some work done before we had time to go find you."

"Isn't it illegal to leave a crime scene?"

"Everywhere else, yes. Here? Well, I know you aren't stupid enough to kill someone and then report finding their leg."

I turned and walked away.

"Lark? Where you off to? I'm afraid that now that I'm here I need you to stay."

"I'm going to go clean."

"Clean what?"

"What do you think? My garage. So karma doesn't give me another leg up."

Made in United States
Orlando, FL
01 August 2023

35639814R00168